T0365531

PROJECT GENESIS

The Gathering

BOOK ONE OF THE PROJECT GENESIS SERIES

W. B. STILES

THE GATHERING
BOOK ONE OF THE PROJECT GENESIS SERIES

This is a work of fiction. All characters, names, incidents, organizations, and dialogue in this novel are either the products of the author's imagination or are used fictitiously.

iUniverse books may be ordered through booksellers or by contacting:

iUniverse
1663 Liberty Drive
Bloomington, IN 47403
www.iuniverse.com
1-800-Authors (1-800-288-4677)

ISBN: 978-1-4917-5101-5 (sc)
ISBN: 978-1-4917-5102-2 (hc)
ISBN: 978-1-4917-5103-9 (e)

Library of Congress Control Number: 2014955119

Print information available on the last page.

iUniverse rev. date: 10/16/2018

To Norma Stiles, my mother,

your encouragement was priceless.

Prologue

Long before Christopher Columbus walked the earth, a meteor began falling from a place beyond the earth's atmosphere toward the continent known today as North America. As the mysterious object made its descent into the atmosphere, it did not burn up from the intense heat, as most meteors did. It survived to become a bright projectile that cut through the night sky like a missile with a long, blazing tail. Traveling in a northwest direction toward a mountain range on the West Coast, it moved at a very high speed. Finally, the meteor ended its long journey with a spectacular show of fireworks as it penetrated a great mountain. With the horrendous force of impact, it burrowed into the mountainside. The lights from the collision illuminated the night sky, and a deafening rumble echoed through the forest. The mountain was set ablaze as the object came to rest deep within the earth. With its great fanfare, this light show was the beginning of a series of events that lead us to the story of the "Gathering."

Chapter 1

Jane heard the car sputter and choke as it slowed down drastically; it was losing power very quickly. There seemed to be just enough momentum in the vehicle to pull over to the curb. Jane was not a mechanic, so when the car died and would not restart, she knew that the only way she would get it out of there was with someone who had mechanical knowledge or a tow truck. She was driving in a part of Seattle that was not one she frequented because of the high crime rate, and she was unfamiliar with the area. It was starting to get dark and looked like it would rain shortly to add to the predicament. Reaching for her cell phone, she saw the blank screen and realized it was dead. She'd forgotten to charge it, and with no charger in the car, her only chance of getting a tow truck was to find a pay phone that worked. To make matters worse, when Jane got out of the car, she slipped and twisted her ankle, sending an excruciating shot of pain up her leg. She hobbled over to the curb and leaned against the car. Sure enough, it started to rain. As the last signs of sunlight disappeared, she discovered there was just one working streetlight on the block. She remembered that she had passed a service station two blocks back and contemplated how she was going to make it to the phone there with a bad ankle. *When you mess up, you do a good job, Jane,* she scolded herself. It was getting dark and raining harder. In this predominantly commercial area, there were very few houses;

plus, it was Sunday, so most of the businesses were not open, and there was no person close by that she could ask for help.

Jane was an attractive woman in the eyes of most people. In her late twenties, she had all the right measurements, a fair complexion, shoulder-length light-blonde hair, and blue eyes. Jane had a small nose, and her lips were dark pink. She was a good reporter and had been on staff for several years, but she probably took more chances than most of her colleagues. She had ventured out there on a lead into the "Slasher" story. The top story for some three weeks had been about a deranged person who was attacking young women with a knife and doing unspeakable things to them with the blade. Three women were dead, and one was in intensive care because of the Seattle Slasher's actions. This was the name people attached to the killer. The police had not yet let the public know if they had made any progress in finding the person who had done this, and the tension around town was very heavy. Jane looked around and saw there were few people walking the streets. Down the street, the only activity she could see was at the service station and convenience store two blocks back.

Jane grabbed her purse, coat, and umbrella from the passenger seat of the car and started walking toward the lights of the station. Her ankle was now throbbing with a nagging pain. She negotiated the sidewalk with a noticeable limp. She was not moving fast, but she figured she would get to that phone one step at a time. After thirty painful steps, Jane stopped to lean against a light pole. She noticed in the poor light the address of a dilapidated two-story apartment building on the same side of the street she was walking down. Then she remembered, 8747 North East. She asked herself, *Is that the address I was looking for?* Wanting to double-check the address, Jane reached into her purse and withdrew the envelope that contained the note that had sent her there. The note showed that the address was correct. Jane put the note in the envelope and slid it back into her purse. The note had read: "I have some information about the Slasher. Meet me this Sunday evening after dark. Ask for Jack in apartment 5. Come alone or no talk." She thought about keeping her appointment but was troubled about approaching the apartments alone and in pain, and then she reasoned in her mind, *This is why I am here: to get information about the murders, and there might be a phone that I can use to get a tow.* Jane had called her story editor previously to let him know about the note, but she got his voice mail. She left him a detailed message that she was going to keep the appointment. Despite her reservations she proceeded toward the apartment building.

The building looked run down, and there was no evidence, as far as she could see, that anyone lived there. As Jane reached the front of the apartments she started to leave, then she noticed a darkened area by the alleyway and a figure of a man standing by a dumpster. He spoke to her. "Are you Jane Watkins, reporter for the *Seattle Gazette* newspaper?"

The man startled Jane, but somehow, she managed to say, "Why, yes, I am. Can I use your phone? My car broke down."

The man moved toward Jane. "Don't live here, just waiting for you. I have no phone."

"Are you the one who left the note at the front desk of the paper for me?" Reluctantly, Jane walked closer to the man, and she heard him say, "That would be me."

"What is your name?" She could barely make him out. She saw that he was about six feet tall with black hair and a lanky build. He had dark eyes in this light, a medium-size nose, and had not shaved in a couple of days. His mouth was slightly open. The stranger was in his thirties and looked like he had been through some hard times lately. He was dressed in a blue sweatshirt with jeans and seemed very troubled.

He answered in a voice that was rough and deep, "My name is Nash, Jack Nash."

Jane was very careful not to get too close in her approach but walked in the alleyway and asked, "Why did you ask me to come here, Mr. Nash?"

"Please call me Jack. I left the note because I know who he is, the one they're looking for, the one who hurt those women."

Jane realized that Jack Nash, if that was his real name, gave this address just to meet her. She was not sure of what he really wanted or how this would end. She saw no one else on the property, but she felt compelled to go through with the interview in this alley with this creepy-looking stranger.

Jane reached into her purse to turn on a tape recorder, which was right next to a .38 revolver that she carried for protection. Jane was certain she was safe for now. As she approached the man, she thought, *At least it is not raining in the alley, and I can finally get to the bottom of who this man is and what he knows about the crimes.* Jane thought she needed to get to the point, so she said, "Who is the one who did those things to the women, and how do you know him?"

"His name is Ramon, and I saw him do those women, every one of them."

Even in this bad light, Jane could see that Jack Nash was uneasy, twitching his head, trying to stay in control of himself. She put her right hand above her purse to have quick access inside. She asked, "Where is this Ramon, and how do you know him?"

He answered her, but Jane could see that Jack was losing his composure in his reply. "He is here."

"Is he in the building or in this alleyway?"

"He is here with us."

She could see Jack was irritated. Jane said, "I don't understand; I don't see anyone else here but us. What do you mean?"

Jack raised his voice. "I mean he is inside of me, woman."

Jane was caught off balance. She struggled for words and then replied, "Are you saying you have a split personality or you are two people?" She could see Jack was getting upset, so she thought she would change her strategy and asked, "Do you want my help, Jack?"

Finally, Jack sighed. "Don't know what I want. I just want the nightmares to stop and this feeling of helplessness when Ramon does bad things. I can't stop him, and sometimes I don't want to. I am afraid I'm beginning to like the awful things that he does … gives me great power and strength."

"I know a doctor who can help you, Jack. Follow me to the phone, and I will call him for you." Jane was very sympathetic with Jack; she thought his problem was psychological.

Jack raised his voice again, "No, woman, I think this was a mistake. You just want to call the police and lock me up."

Jane could see his demeanor change. Jack began to shiver and closed his eyes for a moment. Then suddenly, he was strangely calm, and he opened his eyes and looked right at Jane. She remarked, "No, that's not what I mean. I really want to help you."

He looked right at her and said, "It's too late for that, Jane." Jack had a different, even deeper, more confident voice. He continued, "You have no idea what you are dealing with here. Jack is for me to use as I see fit, then throw away when I am finished with him."

He was no longer acting nervous, and he gave her a look of contentment with a slight smile.

Jane asked him as she was reaching into her purse, "Who am I talking to now?"

"Ramon, of course, I was waiting for the right opportunity to introduce myself. I do adore the presence of a beautiful woman."

Jane was remembering her Catholic teaching about demon possession, and she was questioning in her mind if it was true. She asked, "Do you intend to throw me away too when you are through with me?"

Ramon chided, "Now, why do you have to be so inhospitable to me? I just want to talk."

"Is that what you told the other women you stabbed and cut?" She did not trust this man.

"Again, you use such harsh words, Jane. Where is your writer's curiosity about why these things happen and why humans are so afraid of death?"

"You aren't afraid of anything, Ramon?"

"Well, I am not afraid of that gun you have in your purse or the threats of a woman." He arrogantly continued, "A bullet in the heart of my host is simply an inconvenience until I find a new host, but my purpose in being will not be stopped by you or anyone."

"You are so confident we can do nothing to fight you in murder and violence? You are just wicked." Jane was agitated and really upset about this dialogue.

"It's absurd to think that humans believe you can stop us in our domination of this world, and who are you anyway to say what is wicked? You are not even one score and ten years old. I have lived for thousands of years and have seen things that are beyond your comprehension. You as a race of beings have been favored with a green earth filled with life, and all you do is pollute and misuse what has been given you. It is wrong that mankind was favored of all living things. That is why I detest you so, and we, who are superior to you, went against the ordered state of being. The world will fall into chaos, and we will lead you or destroy you humans. You are a frail excuse for living beings."

Jane could feel his loathing for her. She realized that this was not a simple case of a deranged man acting out his childhood abuse on women. Either Ramon existed as a spiritual entity able to enter a man, or Jack Nash had two different personalities and was crazier than a loony bird. Startled by what she had uncovered there, she realized that she must get away somehow.

"Ramon, are you a spirit or what? What is the ordered state of being?"

"We broke free from the control of servitude, our 'ordered state of being.' No longer do we serve mankind. You really have no idea who you are talking to; I am a god of this world and a being of great power, one who deserves your respect."

Jane was trying to get a clear path to the street, so she could run, but then she remembered the pain she had felt in her ankle and realized she would not win in a race to the street. Ramon was maneuvering himself between her and the street. Something had to be done, or her own safety would be in real jeopardy. Finally, Jane reached into her purse and pulled out the gun. She pointed it at Ramon and told him, "Okay, that's close enough, little god; I am about to fill your host full of .38-caliber bullets. Stop right where you are. Let's see how far you go without a body."

Jane was hoping he would not call her bluff. She really did not want to pull the trigger.

Just then, a sound from a startled cat came from behind the dumpster. Jane turned her head for a brief moment, and Ramon was upon her immediately. He knocked the gun from her hand, and Jane fell to the ground with Ramon's left forearm across her neck. Then she felt his knife enter her abdomen and go upward toward her heart. Ramon talked to her as he cut. "I want to see your soul."

As he reached her rib cage with the blade, Jane unexpectedly felt his weight lift off her body. Blood was oozing from her stomach, and as she started losing consciousness, she reached to cover her wound. Just then, she saw another, larger person hovering over her and felt him put his own hand over her wound. She could feel great warmth in the area of her abdomen, and it spread over her whole body. Life and strength came back to her, and she began to see who it was that rescued her. As Jane's vision cleared, she saw an image of a large man with light emanating from his body through a suit of shining armor. The armor was almost transparent for a brief moment; she saw his blond hair, small nose, and blue eyes; then the armor covered his face again. In just a few seconds, she could feel strength coming back to her body.

"Rest here," he said; then he positioned her so she would be more comfortable. Jane lay there recovering from the attack, not fully conscious yet. Then the man turned to address Ramon, who was supposed to be inside of Jack Nash's body. Jack was on his back unconscious on the ground at the base of the brick wall. He had not moved since the armored man threw him there. Jack seemed to be unresponsive, but the man said to him, "Come out of him."

Nothing happened, and he repeated the command, "Come out of him."

Still nothing happened. For a third time, he said with finality, "In the name of the one who gave us life, come out of him, now!"

The man in shining armor observed a dark vapor come from Jack's nose and mouth, which ultimately formed into a creature that resembled a man, with reptilian features and glowing crimson eyes of fire. His fingers and toes were long with birdlike claws. His mouth was full of jagged teeth fixed in a wicked smile. The man knew he was a dark creature of the shadows. The creature spoke in a monotonic, sinister-sounding voice; he asked, "Who are you that you know about me and can see me?"

"I am life's advocate; I see into the spirit world. What is your name, demon?"

"My name is Ramon, but I have been known by many names. These names would mean nothing to you, except the one some people called 'Jack the Ripper.'"

"Yes, your reputation for terror and murder is well-known in history, but you are no longer going to trouble the women of this area."

"Ha ha ha! Are you going to stop me?"

The man in glowing armor answered, "I would send you to hell if I could, but I know it is not your time yet. I will make it fire and brimstone around here for you if you don't leave right now."

"Threats won't get it done, Mr. Advocate. Eventually, you have to back your words up with action. Let's see if you can take a little pain."

Ramon charged the Advocate, producing a dark sword. As Ramon thrust his sword at his chest, the Advocate raised his left hand and created a round golden shield that blocked Ramon's attempt to hurt him. At the same time, with his right hand, the man produced a glowing sword of fire and pierced Ramon's side. The demon screamed in a high-pitched shriek, like a giant bird in sudden pain. The sound echoed in the city for those who could hear it. A dark substance oozed from the side of the demon, Ramon. He staggered back and shouted, "Never have I been hurt like that! Not since my fight with Michael, the Prince of Hosts. What kind of being are you?"

"That is no concern of yours, demon. It is simply time for you to leave, now."

Ramon was still in demonic shadow form and said, "I will go, but it is not over yet. We are many; you are but one. We will prevail, Advocate."

"Be warned, demon; I will be watching your kind, and you don't know the extent of my power. I too have allies who can hurt you and can band together with me to fight you. Do not come back here!"

Ramon quietly turned into a dark vapor and then floated off into the night.

The one called Advocate turned his eyes toward the woman, who was recovering from her ordeal and was almost back to normal. Still in his armor, he walked toward the woman. Her mouth was slightly open. Her dress was torn with blood staining the front. Her blue eyes opened as she heard him approach her.

"Are you able to get up?" he asked.

He picked up her gun, put the safety on, and then dropped it into her purse. After grabbing the umbrella, he gave both items to her and reached down to give her a hand.

As Jane stood, she began to talk. "Thank you. I have about a thousand questions for you. I heard the name Advocate. Is that who you are?"

Jane was mesmerized by what she saw. This glowing figure of a man had just saved her from a horrible death.

The armored man remarked, "The questions will wait. You need to get the police here, if you can walk. Please call them at that place of business down the street."

Jane hesitated. This was the story of her life: a man in glowing armor, like the knights of old, just saved her life and healed her in a dramatic and supernatural way. Jane told him, "I hope I don't regret this. Okay, I will go, but please don't go anywhere. We need to talk. I'll be right back." She started to go and then hesitated for a moment. She asked, "Do people like you have a phone? Can I call you later?"

The man insisted, "You really need to go now!"

Jane looked disappointed, but then she noticed there was no more pain in her ankle; it was healed also, so she hurried down the street to call the police.

The man was glad that Jane had left. Now he still had to deal with the unconscious Jack Nash. As she went away and out of sight of the alleyway, the Advocate's glowing armor dimmed to reveal a man about six feet four inches tall. His muscular build was hard to hide under the dark medium-length coat with hood lying on his neck. His short blond hair and blue eyes could barely be seen in the city lights. He walked over to Jack Nash, who was still unconscious, lying by the brick wall. He talked to Jack, "Wake up."

The unconscious man responded by opening his eyes. Then he looked around and back at the man standing over him. "Who are you?" Jack got up slowly.

The formerly armored man answered, "My name is John. How do you feel?"

"I feel empty inside and powerless and weak. Ramon is gone. Been so long, I forgot what it feels like to be without him. Did you do that?"

"Yes, you have been swept clean from all spirits. You must replace the emptiness with the power of life, or the evil may come back. Once you have been used in this way, you are vulnerable to being invaded again by the evil ones."

Jack was having a hard time accepting the fact Ramon was gone. He looked at John and said, "I guess I should thank you, but I don't know if I like what you did. I feel weak. I have lived so long this way; I am not liking this." Jack paused for a moment. He finally looked at John again and started speaking very loudly and with great emotion, "I don't understand why, but I feel empty inside. I think you can take your 'power of life' and go to hell. I feel full of pain and regret. What good is that?"

John frowned back at Jack and replied, "You don't know what you're saying. You are clean of the evil that controlled you. You can taste hell yourself if you allow the evil to come back. You need some time to understand what has happened to you. Ramon enjoyed your pain; he used you."

John paused and pointed at Jack. He continued, "The pain of torment I will allow you to remember. After you wake up and you are put in jail, you will be visited by the holy man. Remember his name is Eli. He is your last chance for freedom from the evil. Listen to him. I will ask him to see you."

As John gestured with his hand, Jack screamed in anguish and then fell again unconscious to the ground. John could now hear the sound of police sirens headed his way. He looked around the alleyway and closed his eyes as if to make a mental sweep of the area. After that, he opened his eyes. He began to rise slowly into the air and fly away into the night. Jack was on his back on the ground unconscious when the police arrived.

Chapter 2

The lights of Seattle could be seen in the background from the top of a tall building as a young lady in her teens worked her way to the edge of the structure to look over the side. The teenage girl was a little overweight. She had dark hair that hung down to her shoulders. She had gray eyes, with a small nose and mouth, and was wearing a flowered dress with a long blue coat. It was raining very lightly as she put her foot on the steps that reached to the edge. Looking at the city lights, she was afraid of the action she was considering. A voice in her head said, "Go ahead and jump. No one cares for a fat girl in braces. All you get is ridiculed, and no one understands you and the pain you feel. You have no friends, and your family only laughs at you and criticizes you for liking to eat." She hesitated and thought about the fight that she had gotten into with her mother about losing weight and improving her schoolwork. Her grades suffered dearly from all the emotional stress she was feeling, and her sense of self-worth was nonexistent. No one cared, she reasoned. And the voice in her head said, "Do it! Jump! It will give you the peace you are seeking. They will be better off without you."

As she moved closer to the edge and gathered her courage to end her life, she heard a man's voice behind her say, "It is a lie what you hear in your mind. There is no peace in suicide; you are opening a door that you don't want to go through."

She turned and saw a man in a hooded coat about ten feet from her. He pulled his hood down, and with a look of compassion in his blue eyes, he told her, "You are being deceived in your mind; the truth is clouded by your deep emotional hurt."

The girl looked surprised and asked, "What do you know? You don't know me. You look like one of those beautiful people that everything goes right for. You can't understand what I am feeling."

The hooded man asked her, "What is your name?"

"My name is Cynthia. Why do you act like you care about me? The world would be better off if I was not around."

"You don't have the whole story here, Cynthia. Look in the mirror of potential, and you will see what I am talking about."

The man then raised his hand and moved it in a circular motion to reveal a golden mirror with her reflection inside. The image morphed; Cynthia was beautiful and walking down to the front of the church in her wedding dress with her arm in her father's arm. He had a look of pride and love on his face. Then she saw her first baby in her arms. "It's a girl!" she heard from the nurse. She looked at her daughter with great satisfaction. Next she was walking on a sunny day in a park as an older person enjoying the sights with her husband holding her hand; both had a look of joy and contentment. The mirror slowly disappeared, and Cynthia looked at the man as he said, "This is the potential of Cynthia's life. Sure, there will be heartache in living, but in spite of that, there is a chance for great joy and fulfilling happiness. Don't throw it away. Give yourself a chance. The spirit of life will be with you if you desire and seek him."

Cynthia was both amazed and unbelieving. She questioned him, "How did you do that? That was not a real future for me. My life is such a mess. How do I know it is true for me?"

He reached his right hand out and said to her, "Let me show you the being that is lying to you. Take my hand."

She reached out slowly toward the man's hand and then hesitated. He encouraged her, "Trust me."

He had empathy in his face, so she proceeded. She grabbed his hand and felt some weight on her shoulder. It was a dark creature next to her. He was holding onto her shoulder with claws that were cool to the touch. She could hardly see the shadow creature, but she saw his fiery eyes and felt his cold breath as he said to her in a high-pitched voice, "Don't believe it; there is no future for you. Take the easy way out."

She was startled by the revelation of this shadow creature. She blurted out, "Help me! Set me free from this creature!"

The man reached out and swatted the creature away. They both watched as the creature turned into a dark vapor and then vanished into the air. He said, "He was feeding on your torment and would have had pleasure in your death."

She still did not understand what she had seen. "What was that thing?"

"It was a lower form of a demon sent to harass and deceive mankind."

She looked into his eyes and asked, "Who are you?"

He smiled and said with great concern in his voice, "I am a friend who wants you to live a long, happy life. Look out across the city, and see the hope of new beginnings and the start of a better life for you. Your family loves you. Go back to them, and start over. Remember your potential in life, and live up to it. You can have joy if you look for it in all things, good and bad. Life is for the living. Go out and experience it!"

She looked out across the city and thought about the things that he had said. When she looked back to thank him, he was gone. Cynthia looked one more time out across the city and then left the top of the building and went home.

The mansion was on the side of the mountain in the middle of the forest many miles outside of Seattle. The road to the front gate was paved, and it was dark, but there were lights at the security gate that showed a bronze plaque with the inscription "Tomar Estate." A ten-foot-high brick fence circled the front six hundred acres of the property with signs that warned against trespassing. About a quarter of a mile inside the gate was the mansion. It was a brick building over one hundred years old with white trim and window coverings and twenty rooms. Inside, two old friends were having a glass of wine in the library. One man stood with his glass of wine looking out the window. His long dark hair was turning gray and was tied back, as Native Americans did in that part of the Northwest. He was the taller of the two, about six feet two inches, with a strong brow, high cheekbones, a slender build, and a ruddy complexion. He had dark-brown eyes and a medium-size nose and mouth with no beard or mustache. He was a robust-looking man, who seemed like he would be at home in the outdoors. The other man was a contrast—much shorter, about five feet nine, stoutly built with a light complexion, short brown hair, dark-blue eyes, a sizeable nose, and a nicely trimmed mustache. He was a very scholarly looking man; he seemed like he would be at home in the halls of learning at a large university.

Finally, the shorter man addressed the taller, "Naya Tomanish, great native of the Northwest, why have you asked me here?"

The taller man replied, "Albert, please call me by my given name, not my old tribal name. It would please me."

The other man answered, "Nathaniel Tomar it is then."

When Albert spoke, he had a bit of an English accent. "So why have you called me from my duties at the university to come here, Nathan?"

"Always straight to the point you are, Albert. I like that about you. I will reveal why I asked you here, but first, I wanted to tell you a truth about this mountain. There is a legend about a fountain of youth in the Americas. The great Spanish explorer Juan Ponce de León in the sixteenth century was said to have been looking for it. And even earlier, there are stories about Alexander the Great and

Al-Khidr, a Middle Eastern sage, and their search for the secret of this water. They all died and never found the water of life. I have proof that this legend is real and the water exists."

Albert interrupted his story, "Now that you have my attention, what has this got to do with this mountain?"

"I have discovered a substance in this mountain that when put in normal water can extend life and give people abilities that some would call supernatural and even superhuman." Nathan set his wineglass down, waiting for a response from Albert.

"What are you saying, Nathan? That you have found the fountain of life, and this mountain is the Garden of Eden? Come now, Nathan. How do you expect me to believe that incredible story?"

Albert broke eye contact with Nathan. He looked away, confused by what he had heard.

Nathan went on, "Not without proof, old friend. That is why I asked you here to examine this substance and find out more about its properties and how it works. You are the only man I would trust to this work. I have waited a long time to reveal this to another person, one whom I have confidence and faith will do the right thing."

Albert looked back at Nathan and then exclaimed, "I don't know what to say, Nathan."

After a short pause, he finally said, "I have three days before I have to communicate with university about my position there. You have that time to show me what you are talking about."

Just then, the door to the library opened, and a young man in a hooded coat walked in and said to Nathan, "I am sorry, Dad; I forgot you had company this evening. I have something I must talk to you about ... when you have time."

Nathan smiled and then replied, "John, I am glad you came in. You remember the professor, my old friend Albert Hughes?"

"Why, yes, I remember you from a long time ago. You helped my father with some matters in England some years back. You have degrees in both physics and biology, very remarkable. You have taught at the university for many years. I'm glad to meet you again, Professor. I hope I didn't interrupt anything."

They shook hands. Then Albert explained, "No, not at all, John. I was just about to retire for the night, jet lag and all that. If you can, please, Nathan, show me to my room." Albert looked at Nathan.

Nathan pushed a button on the wall near the door and then said, "I will have Nacu show you to your room, Albert. Good night to you."

Albert replied, "Good night to you both."

Nacu entered the room. He was wearing a tan shirt and dark-blue slacks. He had brown eyes and a slender build. His long dark hair was tied back also in Native American style. Nathan saw Nacu and said, "Albert, you have met Nacu. He will show you to your room. See you at breakfast."

After they closed the door, John said to Nathan, "The professor is a very skeptical man. His thoughts were pessimistic."

Nathan looked sternly at John and said, "I got that feeling also, but then I can only read men's emotions. You can read their thoughts. Be careful with the power that you have. A person's thoughts are private and don't always predict what that person will decide. I have three days to convince Albert to join me in my quest. He is an important ally and a valued friend."

John nodded his head and then changed the subject. "On another matter, the evil ones are very active in this area. I captured the Seattle Slasher this evening. I found him to be a troubled man who was possessed by a class-two demon who called himself Ramon. He was an old spirit that once inhabited Europe, according to what he said. Very conversational fellow. After I pierced his side, he said that he would be back with many others of his kind. It doesn't sound like fun. I could really use your help, Tomar." John affectionately called his father Tomar.

"You did well, Son. What provision did you make for the possessed man?"

"Elias said he would talk to the man, let him know what his choices are. I pray he will make the right decision. What about your help against the dark ones?"

Nathan looked right at John and said, "My priorities are here right now with Albert. His involvement is important to our cause. Increase your efforts in training the new recruits, so we can start using them to help. Aero can be the most useful at this time. Don't use Samson for now; he still has little control of his power. The others are coming along and will be a help soon, I am sure."

John looked troubled by what Nathan had said and replied, "Tomar, you ask a lot of me and my abilities."

Nathan put his hand on John's shoulder. He encouraged him, "You have to see the bigger picture here. There are things working in this place that are catastrophic in nature and could change all things as we know them. They go against the order of things. Help me, Son. You are my right arm. Be strong for me in this."

John nodded his head in approval. "I will do as you say."

A homeless man was sitting in an alley in Chicago on a crate that he intended to use for his bed, but right then, he was enjoying a drink of whiskey from a bottle he had purchased earlier with money from friendly people he'd met on the street. He'd lucked out and got some warm clothes and a hot meal from the mission today. All he had to do was listen to a man talk about Jesus and God and how much they loved him. He could not remember much about that stuff, but now he was having an after-dinner drink. *Yep, this is a good day*, he thought. *The clothes are drab and not very fashionable, but they will help keep me warm, and the shoes I got are great. Haven't had a good pair of shoes for a long time. Think I'll have another drink. Who knows what tomorrow will bring?*

Then he heard a man say, "Is life really good, Richard?"

He was startled by the voice he heard from the shadows. He replied, "Who is that? If you are that preacher man, I told you I am not ready for that Jesus guy yet."

"No, it is not the preacher. Did not come to talk about Jesus. My name is Jacob."

As he came out of the shadows, the man on the crate called Richard could see the other man was well dressed, wearing a very expensive gray suit with a blue tie. He had short light-brown hair, with dark-blue eyes. He had a small nose and mouth and no facial hair, and he carried himself like someone in charge. Jacob was someone who was used to giving orders, he could tell. He had a half smile on his face like he knew something that was important.

"Boy, you sure don't fit in this place. What do you want with me? Have we met before?" Richard asked the man. Then he wiped off his lips, which were still wet from the whiskey bottle.

"No, but I know you, Richard. The others on the street call you Lone Wolf because you like to be alone and don't interact with them very much. Also, you have been living on the streets for a very long time, since your father kicked you out of the house about twenty years ago."

"I would say you are reading my mail, but I don't get mail. How do you know these things about me, mister?"

Jacob walked closer to Richard, careful where he stepped. Then he said, "I am a man of considerable power. Reading a mind is not difficult to me."

Richard became very uneasy, and unbelieving, he said, "That's a cute trick. Someone told you about me, didn't they?"

"No, I am not tricking you. My power can go out of this alleyway. Would you like to know about your sister? Mary is still alive."

Richard was caught by surprise and asked, "My sister? I haven't seen her in over ten years. How is this possible?"

"I see you still require some convincing. You tried to find your sister last year. You went to the old neighborhood, but she was not

19

there anymore and no one knew where she had gone." Jacob paused for a moment and then remarked, "There is no way I could know that, except I have this power, Richard. You see it now, right?"

Tears filled Richard's eyes, and he asked, "Where is she? Can you tell me? Please."

"She is living in California with her husband. Mary has three children. You were the only reason she stayed in this area after your mother died. Finally, she got tired of waiting for you, and when her husband got the promotion, they moved. She gave up on you, just like everyone who is close to you does."

"You got no business in my head. Leave me alone. Why are you messing with me? Life isn't bad enough?" Richard was visibly upset by this time. With his head down, he blurted out, "I wish I was dead. Everyone would be better off without me." Still looking at the ground, he added, "I am so tired of hustling to stay alive."

Jacob nodded his head slowly up and down, and he looked concerned. Then he told him, "Now that is a wish I can honor for you. If you are serious about what you said, give me your hand. I will make it as painless as possible. It is within my power."

Then Jacob reached out toward Richard. Jacob looked confident in what he was saying.

Richard pulled back from Jacob and told him, "You're crazy. How can you do this? Will it be painful? What about the afterlife and God like the preacher said today?"

"There is no God. There is nothing when you die, only oblivion. It will certainly be better than this life, and you will be free of this world; trust me."

Jacob looked like he cared. He reached toward Richard again. Finally, Richard touched Jacob's hand, and then he held on tight as he felt his life force trembling in his body. It was too late now to change his mind. The shock of what was happening was too great. Jacob was absorbing his bodily life force into his being, and after a few moments, he watched as a vapor that looked like Richard's soul left his body and floated away. Richard's eyes closed and sank back into the eye sockets of his lifeless body. Jacob closed his eyes to savor the pure power he felt surging through his being. He let go at last, and Richard's corpse fell to the ground at the base of the crate that he had been sitting on. Looking pleased, Jacob turned to walk away.

It was very dark in the alleyway; Jacob carefully walked toward the street. A light suddenly appeared to his left and began to take a form. It darkened into the shape of a shadowy dragon with reptilian features, claws extended, wings unfurled, and eyes glowing red. Then it changed shape again into an angelic creature dressed in an off-white robe with a red belt. His hair was dark, about medium length. His eyes were glowing; then they turned black as coal, and he looked at Jacob as the light dimmed. Jacob respectfully bowed his head and said, "Master Rafar, how can I help you?"

Jacob looked up at the being when Rafar spoke. "Jacob Starr, leader of men and commerce, I see you went for a little drive tonight, cleaning things up in this city."

"It is my duty in life to clean mankind of the undesirable and weak, but that surely is not why you have graced me with your presence, Lord Rafar."

"No, it is not. As much as I enjoy watching you at work, I have something else to talk to you about." Rafar walked closer toward Jacob and said, "There is an area in the bowels of the earth where my brothers are in prison, a place called Tartarus. If your teaching is complete, you have knowledge of this place. Beings of great power are there and at the right time will be set free. However, none of the ancient ones can go there to free them. A column of eternal fire, which we cannot get through, prevents us."

"Yes, I have heard of this place. The record of it is found in the Book of Sargon of the ancient writings of Babylon. No man, as far as I know, has ever been there."

Rafar nodded his head. "Perhaps you can succeed where we cannot and free those in prison when the time is right. We will need them to secure the earth. Your destiny is at hand, Jacob. But I will talk to you later about this. Right now, you need to grow in power and influence among men."

Jacob bowed his head again and said, "You honor me with your confidence in my abilities. I am at your service, Lord Rafar."

Rafar smiled, approving of the respect Jacob was showing. Then he said, "You are the best of the sons of men, Jacob. Continue as you have until we meet again."

Then he began to transform into the form of the dark dragon and disappeared in a cloud of smoke and light. Jacob was left alone. As he began to walk toward the limousine outside the alleyway, he thought, *So this is why they have had a mutual relationship with my people, one hundred generations of breeding just to help them free others more powerful than themselves. There has to be a way to take advantage of this situation. I think a little study is in order. It is time to open the old books again.* As Jacob stepped out of the alleyway, the limousine pulled up to the curb. A rather large man in uniform stepped out of the driver's seat and opened the door for him.

Stepping into the car, Jacob said, "Take me straight home."

The driver replied, "Yes, sir." As the vehicle pulled away from the entrance to the alley, the last thing one could see was a license plate that read, "LIFE SUCKS."

Chapter 3

"Jane, I should have your job for what you did. We have rules here that are designed for your protection. You are never to go into a dangerous situation by yourself; you could have been killed! That was a very foolish thing to do. And the story about the man in shining armor? What am I to do with that? No one will believe it; this is not the *Enquirer*. I can't print things like that."

The woman behind the desk talking to Jane was an experienced newspaperwoman in her forties. She was dressed in a dark-gray suit, and her short dark-brown hair was pulled back. Her eyes were gray. Her complexion was light. She had an ordinary nose and mouth with light-red lips and a strong chin. She was head editor and very upset with Jane.

Looking disappointed, Jane replied, "Alice, you can't kill this story; it is the biggest one of my life, and as strange as it sounds, it is all true."

"Then clean up the story, no supernatural knights in shining armor. If it is true, then make me a believer. Get me proof this guy exists. Meanwhile, concentrate on the Slasher, Jack Nash. Let that be the meat of this story." Alice was getting louder. The pictures on the wall were starting to vibrate. She was a person who did not get where she was in the news business by mincing words.

Jane stuttered, "B-b-but, Alice—"

Alice interrupted with intensity, "But nothing! Last time I looked at my door, it said Alice G. Miles was the head editor around here. Now leave my office and get to work!"

Jane conceded, "Yes, ma'am."

She grabbed her purse and left. As Jane left the office, she thought to herself, *What does the G. stand for, Grouch?*

Jane hesitated for a moment outside the office. She was still shaken by the previous night's events and was trying to sort it all out.

As Jane rounded the corner in the hallway, she was still reflecting about what had happened when she saw a man in a dark-blue suit with a light-gray shirt and no tie walking toward her. He had dark hair and gray eyes with a large chin. She recognized him as Detective Jones of the Seattle Police Homicide Division. She had talked to him for a short time the previous evening. He said, "Hello, Ms. Watkins, do you have a moment to talk? I need to ask you a few more questions."

Jane was confused. "This won't take long, will it?"

"It shouldn't. I just need to clear a few things up from last night."

Jane motioned to an open door and said, "Sure, Detective. The conference room is not being used."

After they entered, Jane closed the door and told him, "Please sit down."

They both made themselves comfortable. The detective was the first to speak. "You are one lucky woman; the knife looks like it is positive as the weapon used in the other assaults on the women. Tell me again how you survived a direct attack by Nash?"

"As I told you last night, a man saved me, pulled Nash off me, and threw him against the brick wall in the alleyway. I could not get a good look at the guy because of a blinding light."

The detective looked at her with disbelief and responded, "I thought you were hurt last night because of all the blood, but the paramedic said you were not hurt. I don't understand, with all the blood on your dress and on the ground, how it is you were not harmed? The lab says it is your blood type. How is this possible, Ms. Watkins?"

"Look, Detective. Nash assaulted me, and I was bleeding badly. When the man who saved me from his attack touched me, I quit bleeding and felt better."

He gestured with his hands in unbelief and said, "I must say, what a story! Hard to believe!"

"You and my editor should compare notes. She had the same reaction."

"Well, it is hard to understand. All the evidence points to you being stabbed, but there is no physical mark on your body."

Jane looked frustrated with the line of questioning and informed him, "I am sorry, that is all I know about that. Are there anymore questions, Detective?"

"Yes, I understand as a reporter sometimes you record interviews on tape in the field. I was hoping that you might have done that last night when you talked to Nash. Did you?"

She thought for a moment and said, "I'm not sure; I may have done that out of reflex. Let me check on that."

"May I remind you, that tape, if it exists, is physical evidence in the investigation of a crime. Don't make me talk to a judge to get it."

Jane smiled slightly and replied, "Believe me, Detective Jones, it is my intention to cooperate with your office to the fullest. I will call you on that."

Jones smiled back and said, "I am sure you will. Here is my card, Ms. Watkins. Oh, I also need you to come by our office today to release your medical records, if you would be so kind. And if you have not cleaned your dress from last night, please bring it for our crime lab to look at."

Jane was short of time, so she replied, "Okay, if that is all, I have a deadline to make with the paper."

They both got up to leave, and the detective finished by saying, "Thank you, Ms. Watkins. See you soon."

Albert and Nathan were sitting at the dining table in the Tomar mansion; Nathan looked at Albert and said, "Albert, I hope you are enjoying breakfast."

"Why, yes, I am, especially your fresh fruit. How do you get it this time of year and so large?"

"I grow it myself in a controlled atmosphere; it grows quite large and very natural that way. I will show you later."

Albert changed the subject. "I thought I knew you, Nathan, but I am amazed at the claim you made last night. If it had been anyone else but you, I would have left, but you have always been very truthful with me in the past."

"Truth is what we are after, Albert. I am sure you will be amazed by what you see."

After breakfast, Nathan drove Albert in a cart to a remote part of the complex. There was a concrete building constructed right in the mountain like a large military bunker. The door was solid steel, and the access required a hand swipe by Nathan. They entered a large, well-lighted hallway that was very long. They came to a door marked "Environmental Room 001." As they entered through the door, there was another hallway about twenty feet long that terminated at a door marked "The Room." About ten feet down the hallway, there was a door marked "Control."

Nathan said, "We can observe everything in here."

As they went into the control room, Albert noticed the huge window that looked down on a large, sunken exercise room with some very unusual exercise equipment. Nathan went over to a control panel and turned up the sound so they could hear the conversation of the six occupants in the room.

They were all working on different exercises, except John, who was supervising what was going on.

Albert asked, "Nathan, what are they doing? And what is so special about this group of people?"

"Well, you take the man in the corner in the yellow jumpsuit running on the treadmill. You see the numbers on the lighted board above the equipment? As you can see, it says 356." The man was about six feet tall with dark-brown hair and looked to be in his thirties.

Albert looked in that direction and said, "Yes, I do."

"Well, that is 356 miles per hour; he can maintain that for over three hours."

Albert looked astonished. "Remarkable! I don't see his legs; they are a blur."

"Yes, he wore out the mechanical treadmill we had, so I had a company in Europe design one that runs on air with very little friction. I just asked him to keep it under the speed of sound. Don't want a sonic boom in the building. We need to get him on the salt flats in Utah. Give him some running room. His name is Phillip Black; his code name is Aero. He is from Sydney, Australia."

Nathan continued, "Next, we have Carol Saboya in the spotted uniform. Her code name is Jag. You can see how easily she handles the obstacle course. That was a ten-foot barrier she just jumped with ease. She is faster, more agile, and stronger than any Olympic-class athlete. She not only has great physical skills, but she can communicate with animals on some telepathic level. Carol was studying the life in the Amazon in Brazil when I found her with her pet jaguar. She also is a doctor of veterinary medicine and knows a great deal about animals. She was born in Brasilia, Brazil." Carol was about five feet ten inches tall with black hair and was very swift in her movements.

"Looks like you have an international group of people."

Nathan smiled and said, "That is very observant of you. The next special person is Aiko Sakura. You can see her in blue sparring with her brother Hiroki, who is in red. They both are experts in martial arts. Aiko's code name is Siphon, because she can turn the energy around her into other forms of energy or into pure force, making her much more difficult to subdue than her small size would lead you to believe. Her brother Hiroki Sakura is gifted with the ability to heat the air around him to allow him to fly. He can also heat objects to great temperatures and throw flames from his body. We haven't fully tested the limits of his powers yet. His code name is Sol. They both are from Tokyo, Japan." Aiko was about five feet four inches tall with a slender build, and Hiroki was five feet eight inches tall with a muscular build. They both had dark-brown hair. They were on a large mat made for sparring.

As Albert watched the people in the exercise room, he was amazed at the abilities of this group. He finally asked, "It is remarkable what you say and what I have seen so far. What about the big gentleman in the corner in green? What is his special ability?"

"That's Samuel Touré. He is from the Republic of Guinea in Africa. I went to Africa looking for a man who saved another man's life by lifting a truck that weighed twenty tons off him. That was Samuel. See the machine he is doing reps on? He is lying on a bench pushing a bar above his body just with his arms. You see the lighted gauge on the weight machine that he is using? It says five thousand. Well, it is calibrated in pounds, so he is lifting the same weight as two Volkswagens. His code name is Samson; I think you can understand why." Samuel was the largest of the group. He had a dark complexion and very muscular body, which was visible, as he wore a tank top and shorts.

Albert shook his head and said, "Remarkable! That leaves your son, John. What is his special ability?"

"John is the most amazing person I have seen with special abilities. He has superstrength and lightning-fast reflexes; he's the best I have ever seen in hand-to-hand combat, and he has the power of telekinesis—that is, he can create force fields, lift things, and fly at great speeds. He can share his life force with others, resulting in healing and strengthening of other people. And he is the most powerful telepath I have ever met." John was standing near Samuel, wearing an athletic jumpsuit and watching the setting on the weight machine.

"You mean he can read minds?"

"Yes, and control them, to a certain degree. He must remain disciplined in this area, or he could cause damage to another's thought processes. I have tried to teach him to respect others' thoughts and privacy. The remote location here helps him to concentrate away from people, and his room is insulated in lead because it seems to block most mental probes and give him a good night's sleep."

Albert remarked, "Sounds like a blessing and a curse."

Nathan agreed. "So it is, with great power comes great responsibility, Stan Lee 1962."

"I am David Spencer, and this is Steven Ricker. We are from the University of Washington," said David as they walked toward the US park ranger at Mount Rainier's Mowich Lake Camp.

The park ranger shook their hands and said, "My name is Ron Rodriguez. It is kind of cold for you guys to make the trip."

They were all dressed in winter clothes, as it was getting very cold on the mountain; even though it was early summer, winter was not quite over yet up there. The ranger continued, "They just opened this road for the four-wheel drive vehicles. What brings you guys up here?"

David Spencer answered, "Well, Mr. Rodriguez, we have been monitoring a lot of unusual seismic activity on this mountain and wanted to investigate it for ourselves."

The ranger responded, "Call me Ron. May I call you David and Steven?"

David and Steven both nodded their approval.

Steven explained, "We work with the Pacific Northwest Seismic Network to keep a watch on the old volcanoes to make sure they don't wake from their sleep. If Mount Rainier blew its top, it would be much more disastrous than Mount Saint Helens. There are too many large communities near it."

Ron looked very surprised and said, "Sounds like you guys are serious."

David continued, "Yes, I'm afraid so. May be nothing, but we can't afford to take a chance."

Ron motioned toward the ranger station and said, "It's cold out here, and according to the weather service, we are going to get a late-season storm soon, so come into the station. I will get you a cup of coffee, and you can tell me more."

David and Steven agreed and followed the ranger into the building.

In the control room, Albert looked at Nathan and said, "Can I see more of a demonstration of their powers?"

"Sure. Let's start with Samson."

Nathan clicked a switch and used a microphone to say to John, "Test Samson. Let's see how much he can lift today."

John nodded and went over to Samuel. He tapped him on the shoulder to stop him from doing the bench press of five thousand pounds. John repositioned the weight machine so twenty thousand pounds of force was now exerted on the bar in a dead lift position six inches off the ground. Everyone stopped what he or she was doing to watch. Samuel took his six-foot-eight-inch frame over the bar and reached down to grab it with the weight of a Mack truck on it. He was a very muscular, powerful-looking man, but it would take more than his looks to lift this weight. His muscular, dark-brown arms strained to pull the bar into the air. Slowly, with great effort, he lifted the twenty thousand pounds from a floor position to two arms fully extended above his head.

John signaled to Samuel and said, "Hold it. I am going to increase the weight. Tell me when you have had enough."

Samuel nodded to go ahead. John turned the knob to increase the weight—21 … 22 … 23 … 24 … 25 … 26 … 27 … 28 …

29 ... 30,000. It was climbing. Samuel seemed to handle it with some discomfort and straining. One could hear the hydraulics of the machine shifting more weight to the bar. Still the bar remained high above his head.

Albert's eyes were wide open. He said, "He is growing. That's remarkable! He must be over seven feet tall and bigger in size."

Nathan nodded and replied, "Yes, his mass increases to meet the task at hand."

The gauge showed a continual increase: 32 ... 33 ... 34 ... 35 ... 36 ... 37 ... 38,000. Samuel looked strained but nodded for John to increase it more. Going higher, it read 40,000 ... 41 ... 42 ... 43 ... 45,000. Samuel was now over eight feet tall and had to weigh over five hundred pounds. Still, he nodded to go on. As John turned the knob, Samuel looked very tired at 48,000 pounds; he had maintained a great effort for over fifteen minutes.

John waved at Samuel and said, "Can you go on?"

Samuel nodded yes. Finally, it reached 50,000 pounds of pressure.

John remarked, "Well done, Samuel! That's the most you have ever done."

Then John reached over to shut it down. Samuel looked both disappointed and relieved when the weight left and went to zero. Samuel immediately began to reduce in size to his normal six-foot-eight-inch frame. Everyone cheered and clapped for Samuel. John walked over to Samuel and said, "Are you all right?"

"I am fine, John."

John threw a towel at Samuel and said out loud so all could hear, "Let's break for lunch."

They all left the room to go to eat, congratulating Samuel in his astounding feat.

Albert had watched the whole thing from the control room and said, "How is this possible? I don't believe my eyes."

"Believe it, Albert," Nathan said. "It is, as I said; it comes from the substance in this mountain. Study it for me. I have a laboratory set up for you to work. Tell me why it does what it does. No one I have ever met is as qualified as you to scientifically investigate the most amazing substance in the world. You can name it and unlock its secrets."

Albert looked at Nathan and then gazed at the empty exercise room. "I wish Martha was still alive to see this. She always shared in my work. I miss her—buried myself in work after I lost her. She always believed in me, said I was created for a great purpose."

After a moment, Albert turned toward Nathan and said, "I will call the university and tell them I will be spending some time in the great Northwest. I will need to see that laboratory. I am sure you haven't set it up properly for my needs, but I am certain that can be corrected."

Albert reached toward Nathan. He smiled, reached out his hand also, and shook Albert's.

"Thank you, Albert," he said, "for joining me on this journey. I hope it is a very fruitful relationship. Let's get some lunch and meet these extraordinary young people."

They both left the control room.

David Spencer and Steven Ricker from the University of Washington were about a mile from Russell Glacier on the north side of the mountain. The wind was starting to blow harder, reminding them they only had a short time to finish their readings before the storm hit.

David looked at Steven and said, "The carbon dioxide readings are high, there is water runoff, and the ground temperature is higher than expected, evidence that the glacier is melting. Magma must be gathering below."

Steven looked back at David and responded, "Don't put the cart before the horse. We need to get back, discuss our findings, and request a satellite picture of the area. Then we can draw a conclusion based on all the data. We need more readings from other areas on the mountain also."

"Be that as it may, Steven, you don't like what you see, do you?"

Steven hesitated and then replied, "No, I don't, David. It's cold, and I am tired. Let's pick up our instruments and go back down before it gets dark."

They both concluded their work and went back to the ranger station.

Jane walked into the room filled with computer equipment. There was a nerdy-looking young man with wire glasses, wearing blue jeans and a collared, buttoned pullover green shirt, sitting at one of the computers. He was the *Seattle Gazette*'s tech guy and all-around computer whiz, Mike Morris. He was about five feet eight inches tall with a slender build and blond hair. Mike was engrossed in what he was looking at on the computer screen and did not hear her enter the room. He was startled when he heard Jane say, "Mike, can you do me a favor?"

He jumped up from the chair he was sitting in and said, "Hello, Ms. Watkins. What can I do for you?"

"I'm sorry, Mike. Didn't mean to startle you."

"That's all right, just working on something for the weather news. It seems we have a late-season cold front, and they wanted me to check with the National Weather Service to confirm the severity of the storm. I just have to forward the information to the right department ... There, I'm done. What did you want, Ms. Watkins?"

Mike had always acted like he was infatuated with Jane; he got up and offered her a chair. It was evident to Jane that Mike liked her, and she did not want to encourage it in any way. That was why she let him call her Ms. Watkins and not Jane. She asked him, "Mike, I know you are good with the tech stuff; I need to know if you can convert the cassette tape sound into a computer file and analyze it for me?"

Mike nodded his head and said, "Yes, I can copy it in real time and create a WAV file to be analyzed for you. And I can make copies on CD also."

Jane smiled at Mike and gave him the cassette tape. "Great!" she said. "I want three copies, and please can you keep this confidential at this time? This has the sound from the Slasher incident on it. I want to review what happened that evening."

"Wow, Ms. Watkins! That's hot stuff, like investigative work. I can start right away. I should have something for you in a couple of days."

Jane politely insisted, "I need the cassette tape right away. The police want it for their own investigation. Can you give it back to me in the morning?"

Mike nodded his head again and said, "Yes, I will copy it right now for you."

Jane thanked Mike and left him to get to work.

Chapter 4

Jacob Starr was on the phone in his luxury office at the top of the Starr Building, a downtown high-rise. His office was facing the northern sky. From the large window, one could see the shadows of the buildings in the Chicago business district area and Lake Michigan with the white clouds floating over as they often did. His office had a massive desk with a built-in computer screen, two couches, a full bar, and a sixty-inch television display on the wall. Additionally, on the wall was a painting of a man walking through fire and some ancient artifacts, including a spear and shield that were not like anyone would see in a museum. Jacob had a wireless earpiece and microphone and was talking to someone. He was standing looking out the window dressed in an expensive business suit that fit him perfectly.

"Professor, you say the project is a success? You are able to induce a desirable reaction from the mountain?" He hesitated for a response, smiled, and nodded his head in approval of what he was hearing. Then he continued, "That's great, Professor Ohm. I will give you an event date very soon. I understand that if I want it done in a short period of time, then you will need the *big one*. I will have it ready for you soon. I'll call you back in two days with the meet time. Thank you for all your hard work; it will not go unrewarded."

Jacob concluded his call and scarcely had enough time to think about the conversation when he heard over the intercom his secretary's voice saying that Madam Scarlet La Brasa was there to see him. Jacob instructed the secretary to let her in. Scarlet La Brasa walked through the door; she had dark-red hair of medium length and wore a low-cut dark-blue dress. She had dark-brown eyes, a long nose, red lips, and a beauty mark on her right cheek close to her mouth. Scarlet had an emerald amulet necklace in the shape of an octagon that seemed to glow when she came closer to Jacob. She had eight rings on her fingers with topaz, turquoise, diamond, and other precious stones. Her earrings had four small crystals dangling from both ears. She was beautiful in an earthy way and walked with an elegance and grace that seemed to follow her into the room.

Jacob greeted her, "Hello, Madam Scarlet, thank you for seeing me on such short notice."

"Jacob, it is always wonderful to see you. You are looking blessed today. It has been a long time since we last met. How can I be of service to you?"

"Madam, you can start by being honest with me. You see with different eyes than most people, and you have a talent that is rare among humans. Please, tell me what you see in my future and keep the flattery to a minimum, thank you."

Madam Scarlet did not look surprised by what Jacob had said but smiled slightly. She answered, "As you wish, Jacob. To help me see what is forthcoming, you must relax and trust me. Please sit on the couch facing the east and let me look into your eyes and see what your future holds."

Jacob called his secretary on the intercom and told her not to disturb them until he called her back, and then he obeyed Madam Scarlet's request and sat on the couch that faced to the east. Scarlet took a chair across from him just a few feet from the couch.

She looked into his eyes and said, "Let your mind go blank, meditate on nothing. Look into my eyes, Jacob."

Without blinking, he stared back at her. She seemed lost in his eyes for some time and appeared to look into his soul. Then she gasped in shock at what she saw. For a while, she just gazed at him.

Finally, she could take no more and looked away. Scarlet La Brasa was visibly shaken by what she had seen. After a few moments, she then looked back at Jacob and requested a glass of water. Jacob complied and brought her some water in a wineglass he had in his bar in the office. She sipped from the glass and thanked him for the refreshment.

Jacob looked at her and said, "Madam Scarlet, if you are able to talk, I must know what you saw."

She looked into his eyes again and answered, "Please, Jacob, have patience. You have the strongest mind and life force of any I have ever seen. I need some time to interpret what I saw."

Scarlet reached into the bag she had brought with her and pulled out a blue ceramic statuette of a woman about six inches high. She placed the figurine on the table in front of Jacob. The ceramic woman figure was kneeling and looking down into a tiny bowl that she embraced in her arms. There was a small, hollowed-out open area under the bowl. Scarlet placed a little candle in that cavity, and then she poured a tiny amount of oil in the bowl. She asked Jacob to turn off the lights and the air conditioner to make the room as dark and free of air movement as possible. Jacob complied; he also activated the automatic window covering for the large window pane that looked outside. The room was very dark. Madam Scarlet waved her hand over the candle, and it lit. A blue flame about one inch high came from the bowl above the candle. Scarlet said, "Jacob, please, sit and watch the flame."

As Jacob sat down, the flame began to grow beyond the fuel that was feeding it. The flame had a single point; it grew about six inches high and began to throw off red, blue, yellow, and green sparks. It lasted for about thirty seconds, and then the flame began to dance and move from side to side. After this, it became a wall and split in two directions and then became a single flame again. It grew to about a foot high. There were images of men and demonic beings in the fire. Finally, the flame turned into a fiery dragon, flew into the air, and dissipated in smoke. They both looked amazed by what they had seen. Jacob reached over and activated the switch that operated the window covering, and sunlight came into the room. He turned to look at Scarlet. Madam Scarlet looked at the table for a brief moment and then picked up her ceramic female figure and put it into her bag.

She then looked at Jacob and began to speak. "Jacob, that was amazing and very visual. You are a man with plans in plans; you have tried to prepare for all possibilities. You have thought of every contingency, or so you think. In spite of what you have done to prepare for all things, the future has a few surprises for you. There is a secret group of people that will interfere with your plans and a man who will challenge you in your quest for power. He is your match in will and strength. You are alike and yet different. He is from your past and part of your future. This man is powerful in the powers of life, and he is skilled in the ancient ways. He will not be dominated easily. Be careful the oaths you make with men and spirits. It is not wise to walk as an equal to the ancient ones. Be respectful of their influence, or you will have the powers of man and devil against you. Much of what I saw is hard to understand and based upon your ability to adapt or change. Having knowledge is great, but wisdom is the father and patience is the mother of success, and they give birth to endurance. Endurance and perseverance are essential and will win out when your power grows weak. The success of your plans is contingent on you, the decisions you make, and how you adapt to change and deal with your emotions."

Jacob listened to what she said and then paused for a moment and replied, "Madam, as you talked, I thought of *The Iliad* and *The Odyssey* by Homer. Have you read them? Do you know the story?"

Madam Scarlet remarked, "Why, yes, I have, Jacob."

"Then you know it is about the king of Troy and the kings of Greece. It is about love and passion and anger and hatred. It is about war and battle, death and life, betrayal and honor. The players are the gods and mankind and the kings of the earth and their armies. However, most important of all, it is about a decision that Priam, the king of Troy, made not to give Helen back to her husband, Menelaus, the king of Sparta. The beauty of Helen, which launched a thousand ships, is useless, nothing in the big picture of things. This decision cost the lives of thousands and brought about man against man, god against god. All this for the sake of the useless emotion love. Priam's judgment brought heartache and torment for both sides. My life is not cluttered with useless emotions, nor am I ruled by any code of honor. I am guided by my own ambition, and it has never let me down. I trust very few and reward even less. This other formidable man who is in my future can be reasoned with or compromised or destroyed; all men have weaknesses. As far as the ancient ones, they have their place in my life right now, and I know of their treachery to man and their own kind."

Scarlet La Brasa looked intently at Jacob as he spoke. Then she replied, "Jacob Starr, you are a remarkable man. You have never been truly challenged in what you seek, but I saw in your eyes that the day is approaching when you will be shaken to your very soul. All your training and talents and wisdom will not stop what is coming. And I am afraid that your confidence in yourself will be your undoing. At the risk of offending you, I must continue. As in the story of *The Iliad*, you may not know why a man or woman would put his or her life in jeopardy for honor or love or give his or her life for another, but it does happen in some. They are led by something more than what you think is reasonable.

"You may be the Omni-child prophesied to lead mankind into a new age, but until you can grasp why men and women worship life and freedom and love, you are wanting and not complete in your knowledge of mankind. I finish my reading by telling you that the flame went out by itself. That is not a good sign with most people. However, with you, who knows? It could mean a change in direction or purpose. I really don't know. You are unique as a sentient being and beyond normal interpretations. This is my interpretation and reading of your future."

Scarlet La Brasa watched Jacob to see his reaction. He was looking at the empty table where the ceramic woman figure had stood, but he remained without emotion or comment. After a brief moment, she continued, "Is there anything else that I can do for you, Jacob?"

After a short time, Jacob looked at her and responded, "Your honesty is refreshing. Very few speak to me as you have. You have nothing to fear from me, but I am indebted to you, for I have much to meditate about. A wise man uses what works in life and casts away what does not work. I will go into my future with my eyes open, thanks to you. I have always relied on my abilities to get what I must; perhaps I will reconsider that approach in the future. I have never met my equal. It is exciting to think that someone could challenge me in my power. So be it; I have not operated in fear thus far. Even so, I have been lazy since I overcame every mentor and teacher and challenge that my people have brought to me and became the master of all, or so I thought. You have earned my respect, Madam Scarlet La Brasa."

Jacob went to the intercom and said to his secretary to double the amount in the envelope. Then he looked at Scarlet La Brasa and said, "Good day, Madam."

"Blessings to you, Jacob."

Scarlet got up and walked gracefully out of the door. Jacob could still smell her unusual perfume as she left, and there was a faint odor of the smoke of the flame that had gone out. He walked to the window and looked at the clouds in the sky. *What challenges does the future hold? Where are you, man of mystery? What are you doing at this moment?* he wondered.

John was on a mountaintop. He looked out across the mountain range. To the northeast, he could see Mount Baker and the Snoqualmie National Forest. To the northwest lay Seattle and the communities surrounding the lakes and waterways. It was very beautiful, green and lush, except to the south. Guarding over the lesser mountains was Mount Rainier, more than fourteen thousand feet high and still covered with snow, even in summer, all the way to the pointed peak. The great mountain was clothed in clouds at the moment. John loved the Northwest and the majesty and magnificence of it all. No artist could do this justice or poets tell the story of the grandeur and splendor of nature in this part of the world. The sky was still filled with clouds, and the wind was blowing, but the worst of the storm seemed to be over. It had deposited snow at the higher elevations and rain everywhere else.

John stood on the mountain in his hooded coat, looking over nature's handiwork. He came there to clear his head and think about the events of the present. He had a lot to think about—the professor's inclusion in the group, the training of the gathering of people, and the mysteries of why Tomar had put this group together. He lost himself deep in thought. Suddenly, he took a long breath, closed his eyes, and smiled to himself. He opened his eyes again.

John watched the sun peek through a small opening in the clouds, and he heard the cry of a hawk flying nearby. He realized it was midmorning and he must get back to the complex. The professor wanted to interview him about the group and get to know everybody. John looked around at the scenery one more time and relaxed. He smiled again and then gradually went into the air and flew in the direction of the Tomar Estate complex.

In the *Seattle Gazette* computer room, Mike was pleased with the recording of the cassette that Jane gave him; however, he was troubled by what he had heard. He had done as Jane asked. He'd put the sound from the cassette on the computer and listened intently to the sounds from the encounter with the Slasher. Some of the dialogue was hard to hear inside Jane's purse, but he could amplify it and get a good read on what was said. And when Jane was attacked and the purse fell, he could hear a man's voice but no answer. It sounded like he was having a one-sided conversation and getting no reply. Very strange was the lack of sound and the one man talking to … what? He did not know. He needed to do an electronic investigation of the sounds. Suddenly, Jane walked into the room and startled Mike by saying, "Hi, Mike. Is it done?"

"Why, yes, Ms. Watkins, I am finished."

She was excited. "Did you hear it all?"

"Yes, except for some anomalies in the sound, it seems to show that there was more than just you and Nash there. Is it what you are expecting to hear?"

She smiled and said, "Yes, that is what I told the detective and Alice Miles, our grouchy editor."

Jane then smiled again and asked him, "Please remember to keep this quiet until I can sort out a few things about the incident, okay?"

"Sure. A promise is a promise. There are your copies on CD, and here is the original cassette. I have it on my computer now for further analysis or copies, Ms. Watkins."

She grabbed the copies and cassette and then said, "Thanks, Mike. I have to go to the police now. I appreciate what you did. Maybe we can work together on this later."

Mike smiled. He looked surprised and stuttered, "Oh, oh, okay, Ms. Watkins."

Jane threw the CDs and tape in her purse and hurried out of the office. Glancing back at Mike, she waved good-bye. Mike was even more determined to solve the mysteries of the sounds of that eventful day right after he finished the other duties he had to complete for the paper. He left the office in a hurry to fix the network problem they had in the classifieds news office first.

The professor was organizing his lab when John walked in. The door was open, and Albert was standing at a table in the back of his lab. John walked in and announced his presence. "Hello, Professor." Albert pointed at an open door to his office and replied, "Please go into my office. We'll have more privacy there. I will be right with you, John."

As John walked in, he noticed there was not much in the room except a modest-size desk made of ash wood and a few chairs. On the desk was a picture of a pleasant-looking woman with a contagious smile. She was wearing a light-blue dress and had dark hair just past her ears. Albert walked into the room and asked John to grab a chair.

John sat down and asked, "Professor, is that your wife?"

"Yes, that would be Martha." Albert paused for a moment as he sat down behind the desk and then added, "She was my partner in life. I lost her to cancer some years back."

John looked directly at the professor and said, "Sorry about your loss, Professor. I don't need to read your mind to see that you loved her very much."

The professor smiled and said, "Fascinating, you could just get this information by reading my mind, but you respect my privacy and my thoughts. How disciplined you are. How do you do it?"

Albert reached over to turn on a recording device on his desk and added, "Mind if I record your answer, John?"

"No, I don't mind. That is why we are here. When I first noticed my abilities as a child, I was confused and frightened of the sensory information that was coming to me, but Tomar, my father, helped me through the early years to filter out the amount of data that was coming to my mind. My hearing, sight, and senses of smell and touch are well above the normal range of humans. It was a challenge to master the five senses that come to all people. When I found I had supernatural senses, like telekinesis and mind reading, it was impossible without my father's diligent help."

"How did Tomar help you through this tough time?"

"He stayed in my bedroom when I dreamed bad dreams—I almost destroyed my room from the nightmares. He calmed my emotions when thoughts would flood my mind and drive me crazy. He would talk to me and settle me down with his touch. He taught me mental discipline and peaceful activities to help me swim through my own thoughts and retain my identity. Who I am and who I am becoming keeps me focused. Tomar showed me that the abilities I have are a gift—not for personal gain; the purpose is far beyond gold or riches or pleasures I could feel. There are realities and dimensions that men and women cannot see but exist nonetheless and influence our very lives. Most people are blind to the truth of this, but it is very real. And I can help set things right in some small way by using my abilities to help people."

"Remarkable. Can you show me those other dimensions and realities?"

"The human experience will lead to them; your wife has stepped into a different reality. Death is not an end, just a door into something else that we fail to keep in mind about the life experience in this world. Eternity is real. As a scientist, you deal with only what you see and touch and observe, but that's not all there is."

John paused for a moment; Albert responded to what he said, "Science has been my life for fifty years with a brief interlude to fall in love with Martha. It is a means to an end that has left me deficient in information. It generates more questions than it answers. If you honestly go down the road of experimentation and observation without a preconceived notion of what the outcome will be, it sometimes leads to observations of which there is no logical explanation. In space and time, in the observable universe, there has to be more. Faith, belief, hope, and love cannot be put into a test tube, and yet they control our very lives. The intrinsic values of all humans have defined them, and that creates the society that we live in. Your powers give you an insight to the world that I must observe. How can I see what you see and feel?"

John glanced down at the floor and then back at Albert. He answered, "It is possible, but it is very time-consuming and you wanted to know about the others. We should introduce you to them first, Professor."

"You are right, of course, but I am not quite through with you. John, I need to run a few tests on you first. Can I draw some blood and do a DNA swab first? Please come into my lab, and we will proceed."

"Sure, Professor."

John started to get up; then he looked at Albert Hughes and said, "Have you considered taking the water for yourself? It may give you the ability to see that which you seek."

"That is an interesting proposal, John. I will think about it."

They left the office to go into the laboratory.

Chapter 5

The deputy walked up to a cell and yelled through the bars, "Hey, Nash! You have a visitor. Pastor Elias says you want to talk to him."

Jack Nash was lying on the uncomfortable bed in the cell. He thought for a moment and then replied, "Don't know any Pastor Elias. Tell him to get lost."

"The man said that if you do not want to see him now, it will be the last time he comes for you."

Jack remembered what the strange man in the alleyway had said, *"His name is Eli. He is your last chance for freedom."*

Jack asked, "Officer, is Eli short for Elias?"

The deputy thought for a moment and said, "Yes, I think it is. So do you want to see him?"

Jack took a big breath and answered, "Yes, I will see him."

"He is asking for the counselor privilege in a private room. Do you want that also?"

Jack answered, "Sure, I'll hear what the holy man has to say."

The deputy took Jack to the meeting room and opened the door. Elias was standing across the room. He was a tall man with gray hair that covered his ears; he had a medium-build and a ruddy complexion. His brow was large, and he had huge dark eyes that seemed to see beyond the visual world.

His clothing was very modest—a T-shirt, light jacket, blue jeans, with leather shoes. Jack was in his county jail orange jumpsuit and seemed very intimidated by this man's presence. The deputy said to both that he would be outside and when they were done, to just push the call button on the wall. There was a table with chairs in the room. Elias walked over to the table, grabbed a chair, and then said to Jack, "Please, sit down, Jack."

Jack walked over to the table and selected a chair with his shackled hands. He sat down and said, "You're that Eli person that the guy in the alleyway talked about, aren't you?"

"Yes, some people call me Eli, and you would be that guy who was possessed by a nasty killer named Ramon, wouldn't you?"

Jack acknowledged, "Yes, that would be me, but he is not in me anymore, and I will have to pay for what he did."

"Looks like you are in quite a fix, Jack. What are you going to do?"

"I don't know; the guy in the alleyway said that Ramon could come back. If that happened, I guess I might get off on insanity."

"Yes, that's right, but next time, he could bring friends. Would you want to live with them in you, tormenting you, or live without them and die a free man?"

Jack shook his head and said, "Right, what a choice."

"Jack, you don't see the big picture here. What happens to you when you die?"

"I don't know—nothing, lights out; it's all over, total darkness."

Elias remarked, "Jack, wake up! Didn't you learn anything with the possession by Ramon? He was a being from another realm, one that is part of eternity. That alone should tell you that there is no 'lights out' when you die. You exist in a different form of being, that's all."

Jack joked, "Great! Maybe I'll come back as something else. Anything is better than this."

"It is written that it is appointed man once to die and then the judgment. You only get one chance at this life."

"Wow, what a killjoy you are! Don't you have any good news?"

"The good news is that you don't have to be invaded by evil spirits, and you can go into eternity free from your past and forgiven of all wrong you ever did."

"What court of law could forgive all that, not only what Ramon did but what I did by myself, the choices I made, the people I hurt, the things I robbed, the lies I told, all for myself. Even Ramon was my fault. I had to have more power in life, so when that woman in the gift shop said the ancient idol of a brass calf would give me power if I prayed to it and asked for help, I went for it, thinking it would give me great influence and fortune. Look where that got me."

"Jack, the court I am talking about is not of this world. It is the court of heaven and is the final judge in these matters."

Jack mocked, "Sure, Eli, you are a lawyer of heaven, right?"

"No, Jack, but I do know the chief advocate there."

"Okay, am I lucky to know you!"

"Look, Jack, you know there is a spirit world. Ramon was a being from that world, and he controlled you. You were helpless until he was cast out of you. Just what do you believe? In what do you put your faith?"

"I believe in me. Can't trust anyone but me. No one else cares. I have faith in myself."

Eli stared at Jack with a perplexed look and said, "How is that working for you right now, Jack?"

Jack looked down and put his head in his hand. He replied, "Not too well."

"Your problem is mankind's problem also. It started at the Fall."

"You mean that Adam and Eve thing in the garden?"

"Yes, that's right—when Adam and Eve believed a lie that they were gods and had control of their own fate. However, they found out differently, like you did."

"You are talking about eating the apple?"

Elias looked right at Jack and said, "No, I am talking about the pride and rebellion that arose in them that shifted their faith and trust in the Creator to themselves. The eating of the fruit was the bodily act of disobedience resulting in a critical change in them that went to the core of their being. It signified the death of the spirit and the elevation of the flesh as the dominant force in their lives and their children's lives, until physical death claimed their bodies also. The cycle of death remains to this day reflected in all nature and the world. Without the influence of the Spirit of Life in this world, humankind would be hopelessly lost."

"You mean there is hope?"

"Yes, the Creator promised Eve that her seed would bruise the head of Satan, the author of the rebellion in heaven. It was the promise of a savior who would restore humanity back to fellowship with the Creator and end the reign of death in this world. That seed would be born of a virgin in the town of Bethlehem of Judea and would heal the sick, restore sight to the blind, and die on a cross rejected by men only to rise again on the third day to new life, therefore, bringing new life to man also."

"Think I have heard this story before at Sunday school."

Elias answered, "Yes, that story would be about the life of *Ye-Shua*."

Jack corrected Elias, "Don't you mean Jesus Christ?"

"Jesus is what the English called him, and *Christ* means *the anointed*. His Hebrew name is *Ye-Shua Ha-Mashiach*. His family called him *Ye-Shua*. He was and is the anointed one sent from the Creator for man and woman."

"Do I hear a Hebrew accent from you?"

"Hebrew, what makes you say that?"

"Because you speak with an accent like a Jewish rabbi I once heard."

Elias acknowledged, "Yes, I was born a Hebrew and a child of Adam but reborn from above, thanks to the Lord *Ye-Shua*. He has set me free from the penalty of sin. Now with his help every day, I am being set free from the power of sin as he changes me and gives me a new heart. And one day, I will be set free from the presence of sin when I can be with him forever and be like him. He said when he left that he goes to the Father to prepare a place for us that we may be with him for eternity when he returns. This is the good news or the gospel."

"Eli, how do I know this is for me?"

"*Ye-Shua* said, seek and you will find; knock and the door will be opened to you. For God so loved the world that he gave his only begotten Son, that whoever believes in him should not perish but have eternal life. The Spirit of Life is inviting you to participate in eternal life, purchased by the blood of *Ye-Shua* for the world and for Jack Nash. Set before you are life and death. Choose this day life, or the evil will be back. You are not alone in disappointment and loneliness. The Creator has provided a way for you to partake in new life. Start over with a clean slate, and begin your walk in the fullness of life that *Ye-Shua* has provided by his death on the cross. Don't reject this gift; it is the one act that will never be forgiven."

Tears were streaming down Jack's face. He looked down with his face in his hands and cried. He said nothing for a while and then responded, "I feel so alone; that's why I welcomed the company of Ramon. As bad as it was, at least I was not alone."

Elias reached out and touched Jack on his shoulder. "Jack, you are not alone right now. I am here, and the Spirit of Life is wooing you to let him fill the void that exists in your life and permeate it with God's love."

Jack looked up at the eyes of Eli, which had intimidated him before, and saw a look of compassion. Then he said, "How do I change and walk in the new life?"

Elias smiled and said, "First, you must understand that this is a change in life. You are turning from your old ways and accepting the leading of *Ye-Shua* and the Father by his Holy Spirit. *Ye-Shua* said, 'I am the Way, the Truth, and the Life; no man comes to the Father except by me.' There is no other way to God. The book of Romans says, 'If you confess with your mouth the Lord Jesus and believe in your heart that God has raised him from the dead, you will be saved. For with the heart, one believes unto righteousness, and with the mouth, confession is made unto salvation. *Whoever believes in him will not be put to shame.'* Jack, do you believe in *Ye-Shua* and his resurrection to life? Can he be your Lord? If the answer is yes, then pray to him, confess him as your Lord, and give him your life."

Jack looked at Elias, closed his eyes, and said, "Yes, I believe in Jesus ... *Ye-Shua* and what he did for me, and I confess him as Lord in my life. I give you, Lord, myself and ask you to change me and help me in my hour of need. Make right what I have done, and lead me from this point on. Help me, Lord *Ye-Shua*. I need you and ask you to take over in my life."

Elias looked directly into Jack's eyes and said, "I sense a change in your will and a softening of your heart and acceptance of the Spirit of Life. You are born from above by your confession of *Ye-Shua* as Lord and your prayer to God for help in your hour of need. You are set free from the evil ones forever."

Jack's will was broken; tears streamed down his face. "I am still scared of the court and being found guilty of those killings. What do I do now that I have chosen *Ye-Shua*?"

Elias smiled and said, "I will help you. I'll get you a Bible and a lawyer and give you my friendship."

Jack reached out and embraced the man who had terrified him so much just a short while ago, and he said, "I feel a heavy weight lift from my heart."

Samuel was standing over the barbecue in the back of the Tomar Estate mansion in a patio area trying to cook when Phillip walked up and said, "Hey, mate, let me show you how to cook some red meat the way we do it down under."

"Hello, Phillip, I think I'd like to cook my own this time. You cooked the meat too dark last time."

"Sam, you like your steak rare?"

"No, but I don't like it burnt too dark and crunchy."

Phillip remarked, "Suit yourself, Sam; let me throw a steak on the grill for the others too."

Samuel and Phillip made room for each other at the barbecue while Carol Saboya and Aiko Sakura were talking at the table on the patio.

Carol said, "Aiko, I just don't get it. Why are we working so hard? Tomar has not made himself clear why we are training or for what purpose."

Aiko answered, "Carol, we must have patience. I am sure it will be made clear to us soon."

"Yes, I left my work to come to this place, because Tomar said there was a greater need here and we had a special gift that must be developed for the good of humankind."

"He is trying to make us into a team, Carol, one that will stand up to anything. And I am happy that I am learning to control my abilities, and now with the professor here, maybe he can explain why we are so different from other people."

"Yes, that is why I went to the jungle to get away from so-called normal people. My abilities frightened them, and they would not accept me as a person."

Aiko agreed. "That is right, Carol. You see, this is where we belong at this moment in time. I feel it deep inside that something monumental is coming our way. We must stay with Tomar and John and the others. I had a vision last night. I was standing in the forest looking at the scenery when the trees were blown away and burned before my eyes. There was a great pillar of smoke and fire, but there was no sound, just destruction. Everything that I could see was destroyed. Nothing was left but the bare ground; then it turned red and flowed like a river. Everything was laid waste."

Carol looked at Aiko and said, "Yes, the animals sense it also. I feel their confusion and fear something is building or coming. It has to be some catastrophic event that we are in place to help stop."

Aiko saw John and said, "Carol, here comes John. Have you talked to him about the reaction of the animals in the forest?"

John was walking by, very close to the table, so Aiko got his attention and said, "John, may we talk to you for a moment?" She gestured by raising her hand slightly.

John answered, "Yes, ladies, what can I do for you?"

Aiko said, "Carol and I were talking and realized that we both feel that something disastrous may be coming soon. I have had a premonition and vision, and she is picking up the fear in the animals."

John looked at Carol, and their eyes met. John did not need to read her mind to know that she had feelings for him. He prevented himself from encouraging any love interest. It was a tricky situation, one he thought might require a direct approach at some point in the future. John asked, "Is that right, Carol? Do your abilities tell you that?"

"Yes, John. It started several weeks ago and is very strong with the critters close to the great mountain. They have been leaving that area gradually, which is not normal this time of the year."

Aiko spoke next. "I saw the forest disappear and burn. It was total devastation. Nothing survived."

John looked down in thought and then back at the women. He said, "It sounds like Mount Rainier may have some problems. I will talk to Tomar, and we will investigate this. Thank you for sharing this with me. Good work. You both will be part of the investigation of that great mountain." With that, John sat down to visit with everyone.

Tomar was in the chapel on the grounds, about three hundred yards from the patio area. He could smell the barbecue, and he knew he had to join the others soon. He had built the chapel with his own hands many years ago, and it pleased him to pray and meditate there. There was a handmade dark wood cross standing about six feet tall on the north wall just below the natural skylight in the pointed ceiling. The sun was shining on the wall, and Tomar was meditating. He heard a slight sound and looked up to see Pastor Elias standing in the chapel near the cross.

"Eli, it is good to see you. How are you today, my old friend?" Tomar stood up from his kneeling position to speak.

"Good to see you too. I always enjoy seeing you and John. Forgive the interruption, Tomar, but I need your help."

Tomar looked surprised and asked, "What can I do for you, Eli?"

"I need the assistance of a good criminal lawyer."

Tomar smiled and asked, "Criminal lawyer? What does a man who can call fire down from heaven need with a lawyer?"

Eli smiled also and said, "Very funny, Tomar. I need him for the man who was demon possessed, Jack Nash. He made a decision to change his life and would like to have a good defender to minimize the damage done through the demonic interaction in his life. I feel his transformation is real and from the heart."

"Very well, Eli. I will make a phone call and give him the best defense that I can. You amaze me with how you work with people. Is your time with us limited? Will you be leaving soon, or do you have time to break bread with us?"

"Yes, I have time. It will be great to see the fine young people you have gathered together again. On another matter, the Traveler is here in the area. This usually means great change or a major happening. I am sure he will pay you a visit."

"I have had a feeling something was in the wind. There is a great move of evil in this area, and he never misses the big events. Do you know what it is about?"

Eli answered, "I have not talked to Enoch yet, but I know that someone close to you today will enlighten you about the possibility of something catastrophic coming soon and you should listen to them."

Tomar shook his head and said to Eli, "Always a mystery you leave with me; it is part of the intrigue of knowing you."

"Even someone who has been in this life as long as you, Tomar, can learn more about how things are to be and what your role in it is."

Tomar smiled again and said, "My role right now is to feed you and have fellowship. Come and enjoy what we have."

Tomar and Eli left the chapel and joined the others.

Jane was leaving the police department. She was noticeably upset. She said, "The homicide unit has three squads of five detectives who work night and day solving homicides in Seattle. You'd think they would see that I was telling the truth when I explained to them that there was another person at the incident with Nash. However, all the detective could say was that it is inconclusive at this time and they would have to look at the evidence more to come to a final conclusion. What a farce. I would write an article about that if I could get it past my editor."

Jane was talking to Mike, who was in the computer room at the paper, on her cell phone. He was the only one at this time who seemed to believe her. She heard the call waiting chime on her phone and looked to see who it was. She said to Mike, "Oops, speak of the devil, that's my editor right now. Got to go, Mike."

It was not Alice Miles, the head editor, but Fred Hembeck, the story editor, calling. She recognized the number. She switched to his line and said, "Hello, Fred."

Fred responded, "Hello, Jane. Can you come to the office? I need to talk to you right away."

"Fred, I just came from Seattle Homicide following up on the Nash incident. I'm a little busy."

"That's what I want to talk to you about. Alice wants to put someone else on the Nash case. She feels you are too emotionally involved at this time. We think someone else can be more objective about the facts in the case."

Jane, feeling her anger surge, said, "You S-O-B! You know that is my story. Why are you doing this?"

Fred was startled by Jane's words. "Jane, remember, me person in charge—you, employee. You are a good reporter, but I don't have to put up with that kind of personal remark. Jane, we just think you need a change of scenery."

Jane was standing in front of the police department and leaned against the building. She thought, *Be careful what you say, Jane. You don't want to lose your job.* She took a deep breath and said, "I am sorry, Fred, for the outburst, but I can't just shut off my curiosity about the case, and it was my work that brought it to the paper. You have to keep me in the loop."

"Okay, Jane, I will brief you on the case whenever you want. You need to come into the office as soon as possible; we have a new assignment for you."

Jane left the front of the building, got into her car, and went to Fred's office.

Hiroki Sakura was off by himself under one of the many shade trees on the Tomar Estate. Aiko walked up and put her hand on his shoulder. She spoke in Japanese. "Hiroki, brother, why are you by yourself over here? What's going on with you?"

Hiroki answered in Japanese, "Sister, you are my flesh and blood, but I still don't understand what we are doing here with these people. They don't understand our ways or us. Their cities are dirty, their walls have disrespectful writing, and the people do not respect the elderly. They speak with filthy words of a sexual nature. I am almost ashamed that I know the English language. It is unsafe to walk the streets, and they eat sugar and junk food. They are strong in pride and weak in mercy. They are selfish people who live in a rich land that they abuse and misuse. We should go back to Japan and help our own people."

Aiko looked with a loving smile at her twin brother and said, "Tomar and John are not as you speak, and there are good people here to help us understand our abilities. You know, if we go home, those who rule will try to control us. And people fear us; our own family is afraid of us and will not welcome us home. This is where we are welcome and can do the most for good. We have friends here who respect us for who we are."

As she talked, Hiroki leaned against the tree. He took his finger and burned into the bark the words "Aiko and Hiroki, children of the fire" in Japanese. Then he looked at Aiko and said, "Aiko, you are so trusting and find the good in people. However, I see the evil in the world and want to protect you from tribulation's consequences. You will be disappointed in life, but I pray it will not be me. I will stay here with you and see what comes until it is clear that we must move on. May the Great Spirit bless our time in America."

Aiko leaned over and kissed her brother on the cheek. She said, "You worry too much. Come, Brother, eat and enjoy such a beautiful day. After all, the sun is shining and the birds are singing."

Hiroki smiled and hugged his sister.

They left the shade of the tree and joined the others.

Chapter 6

Albert Hughes's Journal

The Genesis Project
Log Entry 13.2

The substance I have called the Genesis Factor has shown amazing abilities to affect living human tissue. It is always beneficial to the tissue when in water—cell structure improves and cancers and cell mutations are eradicated; only healthy cells remain. I have not been able to reproduce the substance, but Tomar seems to have an ample supply. Later, I will examine the source of the substance in the cave, but I wanted to look at it in my lab first. Besides an obvious cure for cancer, over time, I think it can change the human body's reaction to all diseases and promote healing of wounds at remarkable rates. My tests at the DNA level have not fully been completed, but the early results have shown a beneficial change on that level also over time. It seems to improve every living human cell. Animal tissue and dead human tissue showed no reaction to the substance.

As for the humans who have been taking the substance for some time, they all are in perfect health. They have no signs of disease or infirmity. Muscle tone and strength are at optimum levels. All abilities and skills are above normal human levels. Although each person has different abilities that are unique to them, some abilities are in common—like strength, stamina, mental awareness, and psychic abilities. The only exception to this is John. He seems to have many superhuman abilities. My guess is that he was a superior human host for the substance before he began taking it into his body. I will test that theory once I know how long each person has been taking the Genesis Factor.

Nathan has not been tested yet. I am convinced that he has taken this substance for many years, and if I am right, he is much older than people know. I have started taking the substance myself and have seen my awareness and problem-solving abilities improve greatly. My general health has improved, and the gout and arthritis in my knees and hips is gone. I expect that I will see other changes as I continue to take the substance.

One question I still have is how some of these individuals do things far beyond any previous known human ability. The energy readings around each person seem to come and go as each one exhibits his or her abilities. My guess is there is something working here in quantum physics, possibly with the zero energy force, which, if true, would give everyone unlimited power potential. What is the source of their powers? More tests must be conducted.

Jacob Starr looked over the Seattle-Tacoma area as the pilot of his private jet was calling the control tower at Seattle-Tacoma International Airport for landing instructions. He was there to meet with his project manager, Professor George Simon Ohm. Professor Ohm was a brilliant man with special abilities, the perfect man for Project Tahoma. Jacob was always looking for a way for Starr Corp to lead the way in business and control the economy of many parts of the world. Starr Corp was already a leader in many industries, including medicine, microtechnology, electrical generation, disaster-prevention procedures, construction, transportation, and many other international endeavors.

The professor was to meet him at the airport and brief him on the progress so far. Jacob wanted to see what Starr Corp's money was getting them firsthand. When they landed and left the plane, Jacob was dismayed that the professor was not there, only Frances Mobley, the foreman of the project, second under the professor in responsibility. Frances Mobley was also called Centurion because he was very special; he had the strength of one hundred men obtained through selective breeding of his people. As he walked toward him with his bodyguard and driver, Jacob was not happy and looked sternly at Frances. "Where is George? The professor better have a good reason for not being here, Centurion."

"Sir, the professor wanted to have everything ready for you. He is waiting on-site for a personal demonstration of the progress so far. I am prepared to brief you on what is going on at this moment."

As they walked toward the SUV in the parking lot, Jacob made a gesture toward Centurion, and he groaned in pain. Then Jacob said, "That is not good enough. Get him on the phone. I want to hear it from his mouth."

Frances winced and said, "I am sorry, sir. I am just following orders. Please, sir, I am in pain; I can't think."

"My people did not breed you to think, just to do what you are told. I will hold the professor responsible for his actions."

Jacob released Centurion from his hold, and Centurion opened the door for him.

Centurion was a big man, about six feet ten inches tall. He was wearing a size 4X dark-blue jumpsuit. He wore his dark hair short on top and shaved on the sides. He said to Jacob, "Thank you, sir. We will take you to the helicopter pad and be leaving momentarily; the copter is warmed up and ready to go."

Jacob put on the provided jumpsuit, and they left for the helicopter.

"Thanks, John, for responding. I did not know what to do with this one. I needed your expertise before the Feds in the Department of Homeland Security take over the investigation. They always screw things up."

It was Detective Jones at Police Headquarters in Seattle. After he spoke, he reached out to shake the hand of John Tomar. They were outside of the interrogation room. Through the reflective glass, they could see the suspect inside sitting at a table, waiting for officers to come back in and talk to him some more. He was handcuffed and dressed in a beige, long-sleeve shirt with blue jeans. He had a short beard and dark hair.

John said, "Detective, may I introduce Phillip Black, my friend from Australia. I brought him to meet Seattle's finest law enforcement. What do we have here?"

Jones answered, "His ID says he is Omar Desenta, a student from Bandung, Indonesia. A traffic officer almost let him go after a moving violation, but he noticed a suspicious package in the backseat, containing what looked a lot like class B blasting caps. He asked the man to step out of the car and called for backup. The watch commander sergeant got permission to check the vehicle and found enough C4 to bring a building down."

Phillip spoke up. "That's military stuff. How did he get it?"

Jones responded, "We don't know. After we read him his rights, he clammed up and wouldn't talk. Phillip, you were in the military?"

Phillip answered, "Yes, I did my time for the service of my country—"

John interrupted, "How much time do we have?"

Detective Jones said, "I can probably give you only about twenty minutes; the Feds are on their way."

John looked at Jones and said, "That will have to be enough. Give me a piece of paper and a pen."

Jones walked over to a desk and grabbed a sheet of paper and a pen. He handed them to John.

John wrote on the paper and then gave it back to the detective. "Ask him these questions three times. Ask him to think about the answers. I will observe him from this room with the speaker on."

"Okay, John. You can stay in here."

Detective Jones walked into the room with Omar, who spoke English, and said, "Omar, I want to ask you a few questions. Listen to what I ask and think about the answer before you respond. Who are you working with?"

Omar stared at the detective and said nothing. Two more times, he asked him, and finally, Omar responded, "I work with Bugs Bunny, Daffy Duck, and Road Runner."

He had a grin on his face. All this time, John was writing on a piece of paper.

"Where are these other people?" The detective questioned him and followed the same procedure, asking three times.

On the third time, Omar responded, "They are in Disneyland."

Again there was a grin on his face.

Finally, Jones asked the last question, "Where are the explosives? Give me each location and type of explosive." Again, the detective followed the same procedure, asking three times.

On the third time, Omar responded. He looked very serious this time; with eyes wide open, he said, "Allah knows if there are bombs, and you will find out soon enough."

Just then, there was a knock on the door. It was Captain Rogers. He opened the door and said, "Jones, the people from Homeland Security are here. They want to be briefed before they question the suspect. They're in my office."

"Okay, Captain. I will be right there. Let me secure Omar here. I will get another officer to watch him."

Detective Jones walked into the observation room. John had finished writing on the paper. Then he turned to Jones and said, "Detective, listen to me; lives are in danger. There are three bombs on Pier 91. The first is set to go off in thirty-five minutes at the baggage drop-off. The second is close, three minutes later, and the third, three minutes after that. I have written the locations on the pier and the type of explosives. Get the bomb squad over there as soon as possible."

Jones looked puzzled and said, "How are they going to make it to that location in time? The traffic at this time of the day around Pier 91 is terrible."

"Do the best you can. Phillip and I will try to pull the blasting caps from the explosives and disarm the devices before they blow."

Jones asked, "Can you move that fast?"

"I certainly hope so. Remember to tell no one of our involvement."

Jones reached for his phone and said, "We should evacuate. I will make the call."

John raised his hand and said, "No, Detective, there is no way to move over two thousand people in thirty minutes."

Jones responded, "If you are right, I need to talk to my captain now. Got to go. Wish you luck, John."

In conclusion, John said, "Jones, one more thing, don't let him use his phone; the bomb can be detonated remotely also."

The detective shook his head as they went different directions.

"Centurion, where exactly are you taking me on the mountain?" Jacob asked as he looked out the window at the forest scenery.

"Sir, we are going above Paradise, between Stevens Ridge and Fan Lake on the south side of the mountain in a remote area. We got permission from the national park to set up a temporary dwelling to study the volcano. Professor Ohm had very little trouble getting the okay to be there. It is our base of operations. Here it is on the map."

Centurion showed Jacob where it was. Jacob asked again, "Has he been successful in tapping into the volcano's destructive might?"

"Beyond my wildest imagination! He can control the mountain."

Jacob was overcome by the thought of controlling a live volcano and said out loud, "If we have success here, then we can build on this and take control of nature itself. I will have the world at my feet, able to stop or create any disaster of nature. The power of God will be mine. People will pay homage to the new power of the universe."

Jacob observed Centurion, who was looking down as he spoke. Without bothering to look into his mind, Jacob asked him, "You don't agree with me, do you?"

Centurion looked up and answered, "Jacob, sir, you can read my thoughts; I think you are in charge and can do anything you set your mind to. I have seen you do it time after time; I am not about to doubt you now."

"Good answer. Perhaps I was hasty in my anger. The project is important in the scheme of things. I must show the world its way; it is lost right now and needs direction, and I want to be the one to set up a kingdom greater than Rome. I will be the answer to the problems of the world, and they will follow. Your loyalty will not go unrewarded, Frances. There will be a place for those who help me in that undertaking."

The pilot was coming in for a landing in a small clearing. The professor was waiting for them when they landed.

Phillip was just about to enter Elliot Avenue on his way to Magnolia Bridge and Pier 91. He was running over a hundred miles per hour and would be at the pier in a few minutes with about fifteen minutes to find the bombs. When he operated at high speed, it always looked like everyone else was going in slow motion. John was flying overhead, matching his speed, and would be there about the same time. They were going to meet in the area outside the baggage check terminal. Phillip arrived first and was looking for John when he touched him on the shoulder.

Phillip was startled. "You scared me, mate. What's the game plan?"

"The lines are full of boarding people. The first bomb is inside a display for free stuff near the baggage check. Omar put the C4 bomb in the bottom of the display behind a wood panel. You must open the panel and remove the blasting caps in the C4. I will keep people from noticing you. You will have only a few minutes in there to find and neutralize the explosion."

Phillip nodded his head and said, "John, we have only ten minutes for number one; let's do this."

They went inside, and John moved in front of the display in the middle of the baggage check area. There were hundreds of people in line. Phillip went behind the display and found the wood panel, but it had screws holding it shut. As Phillip got his utility knife out to loosen the screws, someone sweeping the floor saw him and walked over to confront him and ask him what he was doing. John stepped in front of him and told him mentally that everything was fine and that Phillip was one of the people who worked on the displays. The man lost interest in what was happening and went back to what he had been doing. After too much time passed, he finally got several screws loose and pulled the panel out. He could see the blasting caps in the C4. There was enough explosive to kill hundreds of people. He cut the tape loose and pulled the blasting caps out. He disconnected the timer with about twenty-five seconds to spare.

Phillip gave the thumbs-up sign to John, who knew that he had been successful. He closed the panel and sped off to the next location at the automatic stairs. John used a mental suggestion to everyone and became invisible to those within sight. Then he flew to the stairs to find the other bomb. He knew that some would still have blurred memories of a flying man, but he had to take that chance. Phillip had already disabled the escalator by finding the power supply and shutting it off. He stood in front of the stairs and told people that the stairs were out of order. John could find and disarm the explosive. John knew it was at the top of the stairs under the electric motor housing. He flew to that area now with his hood pulled down. He used his telekinesis and pulled apart the housing by ripping it open. Then he saw the bomb. It was at the bottom of the electric motor. He used his power to levitate the bomb; then he reached down to pull off the blasting caps and disarmed the timer. With the timer shut off at thirteen seconds, he took off to find the last explosive. This was taking too long; they barely had time to find the other bomb.

Phillip was already fighting the traffic on the ramps, looking for the last bomb. John had told him telepathically where he thought it was. However, Omar was not the one who had put the bomb there, so he only got a general area on the ramp from his mind. Finally, with thirty seconds to go, John gave instructions to Phillip to block access to the ramp. Phillip did so by grabbing a man in a wheelchair and giving him the ride of his life back away from the ship. John flew under the ramp and saw the bomb attached to the support with tape. Having no time to be cautious; he ripped the bomb from the support. The bomb was covered with tape. There was no time to unravel it, and with seconds to go, he flew as fast as he could out over the water, thinking he would throw it across the waves, but he saw a small boat in the harbor where he'd planned on dumping the bomb, so he flew straight up as the time ran out.

Phillip and others saw a spectacular explosion, like a big fireworks show, about five hundred feet in the air. At superspeed, Phillip ran to the dock in time to see something hit the water. He found a way to the shore and ran across the water to that location. Then he dived in time to grab the back of a hooded coat. By this time, the police with the bomb squad had arrived to see their handiwork.

"Professor, why didn't you meet me at the airport?" Jacob was standing outside the trailer in the wilderness, talking to Professor Ohm.

The professor looked him right in the eye and replied, "The project is at a critical stage; it needed my attention. I just could not leave at this time. I knew you would want a full demonstration of the project's capabilities."

Jacob lost his look of anger and said, "You've got my attention. Proceed with your demonstration, Professor."

They both walked inside the trailer. To the right were several monitors with one that looked like a structure network; another was a map of the mountain with blue, orange, and red colors across the map. Another was also a map of the mountain, but it had a grid that looked like a schematic with electrical wires and connections. Each operation station had adjustment knobs with numbers from zero to ten. In addition, there was a keyboard and mouse control with several switches below each monitor.

The professor explained, "This is the control room, Jacob. What I have done is use the natural makeup of the mountain to set up a grid of electrical current through the iron ore and conductible elements in the ground to control the way the mountain reacts to the lava flow and hot gasses in the core. By increasing them in this way, I can control the buildup of pressure within the mountain and ultimately cause an eruption or, in extreme cases, blow the top off the mountain. I can speed up the process that would take months or years to happen naturally. The electric charge I am sending through the mountain gives me a digital picture of rock, earth, and lava buildup in the mountain, and the color spectrum here shows the pressure buildup on this monitor."

"What you are describing is a Mount Saint Helens–type explosion, and I heard experts say that Mount Rainer has never had that type of eruption, according to the geological records, with the lava flows, ash deposits, and volcanic mud flows from the glaciers."

The professor said, "The mountain itself has the heavy, sticky lava that was present in the Mount Saint Helens explosion. Those same conditions are also here in Rainer. My process has brought heavier particles to the top, three times the amount that was in Mount Saint Helens, by my estimates. As the pressure builds up, it could blow the top of Rainer right off." Professor Ohm pulled his hands apart quickly to demonstrate this with a gesture.

"How does the megaton bomb play into the plan?"

"I have created a shaft with my abilities that goes to a strategic spot in the mountain. It is weakest on the west side toward the populated areas. When the pressure and the lava volume are right, the proper ignition of the bomb, in my opinion, would cause a volcanic explosion greater than three Mount Saint Helens eruptions. That would devastate the terrain in about a twenty-mile radius with floods and mud flows into Tahoma, south Seattle, and other heavily populated areas. It would destroy the economy in about half of Washington State. The death count would be hundreds of thousands or millions."

Jacob asked, "How long would the process take, Professor? And will there be any radiation from the bomb?"

"Without the bomb, it would take days or weeks to get the right pressure to cause an eruption of moderate proportions. Many would be prepared, and the damage, although significant, would be manageable by the populace. The explosion of the mountain from within and the fact that the megaton bomb would be deep in the earth would hide any evidence of radiation for a long time. The electromagnetic pulse, or EMP, from the bomb would be minimal and not be a major factor. With the bomb, we could have an eruption in forty-eight hours, if my calculations are correct. That would definitely change the landscape of Washington for some time. It would catch many people by surprise."

Jacob pointed at the monitors and demanded, "Can you show me what you can do right now?"

The professor reached for the control panel. "Sure, we can cause the mountain to let off a little steam."

With that, the professor turned the knobs on the console panel by the middle monitor, and the color of the mountain map slowly changed from blue to orange in the core area. The earth shook, and the trailer did also. The professor looked at Jacob and said, "This will take about forty-five minutes to get up to pressure. Let's get a cup of coffee."

They went to the little kitchen and poured the coffee. Jacob had his with two sugars, and Professor Ohm had his black.

Jacob looked at the professor and said, "You know a megaton bomb weighs over a thousand pounds, Professor. Does your shaft have enough room to get the device to the strategic spot?"

"Yes, I checked the measurements. If we take the outer casing off, it will fit nicely in the shaft. With remote detonation, we can pinpoint the time you want the eruption."

About thirty-five minutes later, Centurion tapped the professor on the shoulder and pointed toward the TV, which was showing the news out of Seattle. A news helicopter was flying over the mountain and reporting.

"This is Channel 7 Eyewitness News. We are in our flyby of Mount Rainier and are the first to show our viewers the cloud of steam coming from the top of the mountain. You can see from our camera that the cloud reaches well above the summit of the mountain. It is a reminder that we have our very own volcano right in our backyard. Now we return to the studio to talk to experts about the mountain that the Native Americans called Tahoma."

"Very impressive. The cloud is getting bigger. It is time to make contact with my Portland office to see if they're ready. We have been moving equipment and supplies there for months, so if any disaster happens, we can be the savior for the area and rebuild in the name of Starr Enterprises. This will help us politically and strategically to have a presence in this area for years, and it will wake the nation up to the benevolence of our company. Ultimately, it will be Jacob Starr's open door to power. If we pull this off, I should be able to write my own ticket to any area of influence in the world."

The professor then shut down the demonstration and showed Jacob the rest of the operation. Jacob remarked that he would be staying in the area for a while.

Chapter 7

John had burns on his hands and was breathing hard when Phillip brought him to the shore. The sleeves of his coat were gone, and his clothes smelled of smoke, but he was alive—to Phillip's amazement. Phillip watched as red and charred flesh on his hands and forearms returned to a normal skin color right before his eyes.

Finally, John asked, "Did we do it? Are the people safe?"

"They are fine, mate. I thought you were a goner! Good to see you are all right. You're tougher than you look."

John looked up and said, "I need a few moments, but I'm okay. Thanks for digging me out of the water. Had a hard time getting rid of that hot potato."

Phillip looked confused and said, "Potato? I thought it was a bomb. Oh yes, you Americans speak a different language. I'm glad you got it up in the air and you're in one piece. You're either lucky or very good at what you do."

John got to his feet and said, "Let's get out of here before someone sees us, Phillip."

They left for home.

As Jane climbed out of the Channel 7 helicopter, she thought, *What a step down—from a major story about the modern-day "Jack the*

Ripper" to a mountain letting off steam. What do they want from me? I have to make the best of this. There has to be a story here.

Just then, she saw the Channel 7 monitors in the TV truck with news about Pier 91. It seemed there had been an explosion over the water, and the bomb squad was there. Someone in the crowd took a picture of a person flying in the air just before the explosion over the water. The close-up showed a blur, but Jane was convinced that the man was the same one who had saved her from the attack of Jack Nash. Jane stepped around the pilot and said, "Out of my way! I have to get to my car."

Jane was on her way to the pier, hoping she could get a scoop. She was determined to find out more information about what had happened there. This time, her car started for her, and she was on her way.

The Pier 91 parking lot and shuttle area were very crowded. She had to park way in the back because of all the extra emergency vehicles. By the time she got to the baggage area, they were setting up a staging area in front for the media. Jane showed her press pass and then pushed her way to the front. Captain Rogers was about to address the news people. She looked around; there was no one from the *Seattle Gazette* there as far as she could see. As she looked toward the front, she saw Detective Jones. *He works homicide,* she thought. *What is he doing here?*

Rogers tested his microphone and spoke to the group of reporters. It was very noisy, but people quieted down to hear him.

"I have a statement for the media, but I want you to understand that this incident is an ongoing investigation. There may be some aspects of the event I cannot discuss at this time. This is what we know: A man was arrested earlier in a traffic violation with explosives in his car. We took him to our downtown office for interrogation. We learned that there were explosives at Pier 91 set to go off today. The bombs were successfully disabled except for the one that went off over the water. As far as we know, no one was hurt, but we are in the process of finding that out. We are still interviewing witnesses about this incident and will tell you more when it is appropriate to do so. All loading and departures are stopped until the entire pier has been secured and all people are safe. Homeland Security is involved and helping in this investigation. That is what we know at this point. I will accept a few questions at this time."

The press got loud, all clamoring to get their question asked. Finally, Rogers pointed at the CCN affiliate newsperson, "Is there more than one person involved, and is there any information about another plot of violence at any other transportation place in Seattle?"

Rogers replied, "No, as far as we know, the attempt to cause damage was only at Pier 91, and I cannot answer the question about suspects at this time, including how many were involved."

The news people clamored again to get to ask their question. Jane was wondering if she would have a chance to ask a question. Suddenly, Rogers pointed at the FCX news affiliate.

"Was this a terrorist attack like 9/11, and do you expect more attempts on this community in the future?"

Rogers answered, "We are diligently working to stop all attempts of violence and are cooperating with Homeland Security to thwart any attempt to damage property and hurt people. As far as it being considered a terrorist attack, that remains to be seen."

The people of the press again became very loud in their attempts to be heard so they could ask their question. *Wow, what a chauvinist! Why won't you pick a woman?* Jane thought as she yelled out, "Captain Rogers!" to be heard. Just as she was going to give up, Rogers pointed at her.

She was speechless for a moment and then blurted out, "Someone showed a picture to Channel 7 Eyewitness News of a flying man out over the water just before the explosion. Do you have an identity of that person, or can you comment on that picture?"

Captain Rogers bit his lower lip and then said, "I can't comment on that; there is no evidence I have seen that a 'flying man' was involved in this incident, much less his identity. I am sure there is a logical explanation for the picture, if it exists."

The news people were stunned by her claims about the flying man and persisted in asking if something supernatural had happened at the pier. The question generated a lot of unanswerable questions. Finally, Rogers got frustrated with the line of questioning and concluded the news brief saying, "When more things come to light about this case, I will share the *facts* with the media, not fabrications or fantasy."

With that, Rogers left the area to join the folks from Homeland Security. It was getting late in the afternoon. Jane called her editor and left to get to the *Gazette* building.

It was evening; the sun had set, and Tomar was behind the mansion looking at the first stars of the night. There was just enough light left to see an opossum and her babies in the grass and a squirrel running for a tree before it got completely dark. He was thinking about the events of the day—the near disaster of the explosion at Pier 91 and the minor earthquake and venting of Mount Rainier he'd seen on the news that day. He wondered if it was luck, good training, or God's hand that had kept John safe from harm. He thought about the mountain quake followed by a cloud of steam from the peak and couldn't shake the feeling that something unnatural was going on.

He was still deep in thought when Professor Hughes walked up to him and said, "We need to talk, Nathan. I need some clarification about a few things concerning the Genesis Factor substance. May we talk now?"

"First thing, how is John? Nacu said you examined him?"

Hughes responded, "Yes, I did. Except for the smell of smoke and burnt clothes, he looked great. His flesh, bone, veins, hair, blood supply, and muscle tissue are all fine. His recovery ability is astounding. The explosion must have generated heat of over a thousand degrees, and the force could have brought down a building, yet he survived—not only survived, but his body is in outstanding shape. I think he could run a marathon if he had to."

Tomar agreed. "Yes, he has a remarkable body and mind. Having raised him, I still worry about his safety and well-being. He is very powerful in ability and mind-set. There is nothing he could not do or accomplish. He is my greatest treasure. It has been a blessing to have been a part of his life."

Professor Hughes remarked, "Nathan, I am not a counselor, but have you ever told him that? I regret a lot of things done and words not said in my life. My short life with Martha left me regretful about unsaid words to her."

Tomar shook his head and said, "Yes, it is time to say many things that have been unsaid; you have brought closure to a journey that began many years ago. The work you are doing is revealing a mystery that has been locked up for centuries, one that will answer many questions I have had since discovering the substance."

Hughes said, "The mystery I want to hear is your story, Nathan. How did you find this miraculous substance? How did it come into your life? And how has it affected you?"

Finally, Tomar answered, "Yes, it's time to tell you a story about a young brave from an ancient tribe in this area. His native language has long been forgotten, but I will tell his story. The Puqejas were peaceful people but fierce warriors. They defended themselves well against the wild beasts and other competing tribes. They also were very superstitious and held traditions and tribal ways sacred. Smoha was the brave's name. It means 'dreamer,' and it fit him well. He questioned every tradition and tribal way. He told others of his dreams of flying beings and fire sticks that could harm someone just by pointing. He spoke of peoples across the waters who would come and change everything. He told of great boats and flying eagles with men on them—terrible fighting machines that were very hard to describe to his people.

"The tribal leaders ridiculed Smoha and said he must stop sharing his dreams because they already had a shaman. The shaman told the leaders and members of the tribe that Smoha was controlled by an evil spirit and must be cast out. Finally, the chief listened to the shaman and ordered Smoha cast out of the tribe before his test of manhood. Driven out from his people many miles from home, he found himself near Fire Mountain. It was a forbidden place for the people of the tribe because of the bad magic there. Many braves never came back after venturing to the mountain.

"Smoha made a fireless camp at the base of the mountain. Bobcats, cougars, and wolves lived in these woods. Also, there were black bears and the horrible bear, which is what the tribes called the grizzly, the largest and most powerful of all predators. The moon was out, but it was hard to see in the brush where Smoha made his bed. As he lay there, he could hear wolves howling at the moon. He figured they were not a threat, as they were too far away. He heard the hoot of an owl and the rustle of what he thought must be a raccoon in the bushes. He put on the outer garment, called a *ruaha* by some tribes; it would keep him warm. He also had the knife his father gave him, the blade made from bone and the handle from wood interlaced by animal leather to make it easy to handle. The spear he had was longer than most with a bone spearhead, and the shaft was made from the hardest wood his father could find. As he lay there, he prayed to the Great Spirit to protect him and give his life purpose.

"Smoha feared falling asleep but finally fell into a light slumber. Suddenly, he heard someone say, 'Smoha,' and he looked up and saw a man standing above him. As he reached for his knife, the man touched his hand and said, 'It's all right; if I'd wanted to hurt you, I would have done so when you slept.'

"Smoha relaxed and said, 'What do you want? Who are you?'

"The man answered, 'I am the messenger of the Great Spirit. I am here to tell you what your future holds and about the trials and tests that lie ahead. You have been chosen to walk this journey by the one who created all things to lead the end time gathering and to fight the great evil of that day.'

"Smoha sat up and said, 'I am not a brave and have not yet the trial of manhood. How can this be?'

"Smoha noticed that with the man near him, the forest was like daytime and yet there was no sun in the sky. He was dressed in a robe, which was as white as the snow, and had eyes that appeared like fire with long hair and a medium-length beard that glowed against the background of the forest. Could this man be sent from the Great Spirit?

"The man responded, 'I am he that was and is and will be. I speak truth and am truth and lead the way for all to come to God.'

"Smoha felt his knees grow weak. He fell on his face and worshiped him. 'Forgive me, Great One from above. I am but a young man, not worthy of your charge.'

"The man calmed Smoha and said, 'I speak and make worthy those who are called and will give you strength to do what you are called to do. Rise up and fear not.'

"Smoha looked up and saw him smile. As he slowly got up, the One from above spoke. 'You are the guardian of this mountain and its secrets. You will be tested this day and be called to manhood. I give you this mountain to keep from evil and protect its mystery of life. You will understand more in time, but the first step is to subdue that which is in this place. Proceed up the mountain when the sun comes out, and it will become clear what to do. Remember, I will give you the strength you need to complete your journey. Call to me, and I will hear you. Keep your heart and mind pure; I will give you the power to complete all things.'

"Smoha asked him, 'What shall I call you when I speak to you?'

"'In your language, call me 'Anonius' (meaning Lord Come). Speak this name with pureness of heart, and I will hear and answer you. It has been set in motion; that which is to come is here. Rest now, for it is night. When it is day, begin your task.'

"Smoha felt his eyes grow weary. He watched Anonius disappear and the forest go dark, and then he lay down and fell into a deep sleep.

"Smoha woke from sleep hungry. He found some berries and cool water from a stream. He ate some food from the village that he had prepared before he left, and he ate the tribal version of jerky, which was made from deer meat and berries. As he had breakfast, he wondered if Anonius's visit of the previous night was a dream or real. He felt led to go up the mountain and see this mountain and its secrets. Why was it forbidden to his tribe? He would obey Anonius and see.

"As Smoha began to ascend the mountain, he noticed the grade was not too steep, the trees were not very dense, and traveling was fairly easy. Then he saw a fallen tree limb that had been crushed by something very heavy. He looked around and saw a footprint by the limb. It was clearly a bear print about three hands long or twenty-five inches. This had to be the largest horrible bear or grizzly ever to walk in this forest. Most large grizzly bears' tracks are only two hands long or fifteen inches. This definitely got his attention. He began to study the tracks, hoping for more signs, and looked to see which way the breeze was blowing to discover if his scent would get the attention of something downwind of him.

"Showing determination, Smoha continued up the mountain. The path he was taking opened into a clearing with very few trees. This meadow was fairly level and had tall grass and wildflowers growing in it. He surely could be seen easily by any predator in this grassy area. It was late morning by that time, and the sun was rising. Across the meadow, he could see a cliff and a dark area at the base of the sharp incline. There certainly was an easier way up the mountain, but he seemed drawn to the shade of the incline. So Smoha proceeded in a line around the meadow toward the cliff.

"As he neared the cliff, he noticed the dark area at the base of the incline was actually a cave partially overgrown with foliage. Then Smoha noticed the wind had changed direction; instead of a cross wind, it began to blow in the direction he was going, toward the cliff. His scent would precede him in that direction. He thought about circling around when he heard the 'pop' of a pair of giant jaws, and the deep grunt of something very large running toward him. Then Smoha saw the giant grizzly. He had dark-brown fur with a lighter color around his neck and upper chest area. The bear was charging like a bull, heading straight for him from the dark area of the cliff. He was about 150 feet away and running about thirty miles per hour. He would be on him in seconds, no chance to outrun him.

"Smoha knew that grizzlies like to use their large size to intimidate and bowl over an opponent but something that large could not turn or stop very quickly. So when the bear was very close to the young man, Smoha took off to his left as fast as he could. He ran toward the cliff and higher ground, hoping that there he would find a place of safety. The bear missed the young brave and took another fifty feet to stop and turn around. He then chased him toward the cliff. As Smoha came to the base of the incline, he found sure footing on the left of the cave, and by the time the bear reached the path of his ascent, the young man was about twenty feet up the side of the incline. Feeling safe, Smoha stopped to catch his breath on a boulder on the side of the cliff.

"The bear was not deterred and stood on his hind legs. From ground to head, he was almost fourteen feet. He reached out and clawed at the base of the boulder, shaking it loose. Smoha and the large rock came tumbling down. He rode it to the ground and landed at the foot of the bear. Luckily, the boulder hit the bear on the leg and knocked him down. The bear and young man were both shaken by the mini landslide. Smoha was cut and bleeding; the bear had been able to rake at his side before he fell, and the sharp rocks had lacerated his right leg. Somehow, the young man was able to get up first. Smoha understood he could not get away in his condition, so he stood by the boulder and found the spear his father had made for him. It had survived the fall somehow.

"Smoha knew he only had one chance at this. He braced himself against the rock with the spear in his hand as the bear got up. The bear lunged his large frame at the young man. There was an opening for a brief instant when the bear exposed his chest, and Smoha found the mark with his spear over the heart. Not having the strength to run him through, the young brave placed the other end of the spear against the rock, and the weight of the animal did the rest. The heart of the great animal was run through, and the bear let out a loud yelp and fell to his death at the feet of Smoha. The bear's giant arm knocked Smoha down, but it had no life left to hurt him anymore.

"Smoha was hurting and bleeding; every muscle ached. After a moment, exhausted, he crawled from the side of the giant beast. He thought how his father had prepared him for this moment with his training and the tools of a brave. The magnificent spear his father made with his own hands did not break and was still in one piece with the weight of this great animal on it, and he had followed the instruction of the One from above, Anonius, to ascend the mountain and find its secrets. The young man was hurt, in pain, and bloody. He cried out, 'Anonius, help me!'

"He heard a voice; it said, 'Go into the cave and drink of the water, the mystery of life.'"

"Nathan, that young man was you and the story is your story, right?" Albert Hughes interrupted Nathan's story.

Nathan smiled without answering and continued, "The young brave crawled into the cave and slowly pulled himself up to explore the darkness, but to his surprise, as he walked about seventy-five feet inside, there was an amber glow coming from a pool of water that was fed by an underground spring or water source. The rock around the cave was smooth, like it had been formed by some great force or heat. The light was coming from an object in the pool. It refracted through the water brightly enough to reflect on the walls of the cave.

"Smoha was still hurting, and he started to bleed from the open wound on his leg. He ignored the wonder of the cave long enough to reach down and put his hand in the pool and cup some water to wash out his wounds, but he slipped on the rock because he was so weak and fell into the shallow pool. As he lay with his head above the water, he felt a warmth rush through his body. Strength came back to his legs and arms and then to his back and chest. He lay there for some time—how long, he could not remember—but when he crawled out of the pool, he noticed that the lacerations to his side and right leg were almost healed. He was convinced a few more moments in the pool, and he would be entirely healed.

"What had he discovered here, and what did it mean? he wondered. Then he heard a voice from the darkness.

"'I am told your name is Smoha. Is that correct?'

"The young man was startled and reached for the knife in his belt, which had survived the ordeal. Then he said, 'Who are you? What do you want?'

"The man stepped into the glow of the cave. Smoha saw a man about five feet ten inches with a hooded one-piece dark cloak, a cloth belt around his middle, and what looked like open-toed shoes. The amber glow in the cave kept him from making out the colors of the clothes. He had a large brow, high cheekbones, narrow eyes, and a beard. It was strange to Smoha because the tribes did not allow facial hair on men. He pulled his hood back and said, 'I am the Traveler; it is my job to record major events in history and write them in the books of time. I am also known as Enoch.'

"'Traveler, are you here for a major event involving me?'

"'Well, yes, where you stand in this cave is the largest deposit of the water of life in the world, and you, Smoha, have been designated the guardian of life and have been charged with the duty to protect the cave from man's corruption. It is a high honor.'

"Smoha looked surprised and said, 'I just discovered this cave, and you are here to keep a record of this? Can you tell me the future and what it holds for me? What do I do next?'

"Enoch smiled and said, 'I am not here to give you answers to your questions. I am here to record the events of the day, but I can tell you that this is simply a beginning; there will be many more adventures for you, and to be successful, you must remain true to your calling and protect that which has been given to you.'

"Smoha was confused and said, 'I will stay true to the commandment of Anonius and guard what he has given until I learn more about what is to come. Will I see you again, Enoch?'

"'I am sure you will, young Smoha, for we both serve the same Lord and have been given responsibility by him for his purpose. Until we meet again, God be with you.'

"The Traveler stepped back into the darkness and disappeared from his site. Smoha heard no more footsteps, and his tracks stopped abruptly like he had vanished into the thin air.

"The young man stayed true to what was asked and had many adventures, but through it all, he kept the secret of the mountain from the world. You are the first one to hear Smoha's—or my—story."

"Nathan, how many years ago was that?" Albert Hughes asked.

"I put a small stone down in the floor of the cave for each cycle of seasons; there are fifteen piles, each one hundred rocks deep. It was, according to that method, the year 510 in the Christian calendar or the tenth year of the sixth century."

Professor Albert Hughes concluded, "You are over fifteen hundred years old? That is truly remarkable. What have I gotten myself into here?" Albert looked like he was having a hard time absorbing what he had just heard. With that, Nathan suggested they leave the patio to get something to eat.

Chapter 8

"Jane, your story is a good one, but please clean up the supernatural reference to the rumor about the flying man over the water." Fred Hembeck did not approve of Jane's approach in the story. "Your insistence on printing stories about unproven supernatural things really puts pressure on an editor."

Jane responded, "I am simply quoting the Channel 7 News, and I got a copy of the picture from them." She was still pushing to leave it in the story.

"The picture is inconclusive and certainly proves very little about the ability of a man to fly." Fred stood his ground on this directive. "If you want your story printed in the next edition, you have thirty minutes to redo it for proofreading."

Jane responded, "Okay, Fred, can you include the picture in the article?"

"No, we will feature the picture of the ship in the dock."

"Well, that's exciting!" Jane exclaimed sarcastically.

Fred shook his head and said, "Jane, you have a knack for getting the big story, but you need to respect the job that editors have and accept the answers they give. Now, please finish your story."

Jane left the office and went to her desk to redo the story; as reluctant as she felt, she needed this job, and her rent was overdue. As she sat down to work and took a sip from her two-hour-old coffee, something struck her. She got a pad and started to write:

1. Nash saw the other man in the alley after he stabbed me. I have to see Nash. Maybe he can help me track him down.
2. Detective Jones knows more than he told me about the third guy. I feel in my gut there has to be something there.
3. Mike, the computer nerd, can help me with this photo.

Then she put the note inside her purse and said out loud, "Now there is a to-do list that might give me some answers." She cleaned up the story per the instructions her editor gave and left the office.

Tomar knew the mountain very well; it had been the highest, most-intimidating mountain peak in the Northwest for hundreds of years and had claimed the lives of many would-be climbers. The glaciers were dangerous and very unforgiving to inexperienced explorers. The weather could change and be a great factor in survival, even in the summer. Tomar in his first helicopter flyby of the mountain saw nothing very unusual, except a lone trailer on the south side of the mountain above Paradise. He would finish his sweep on the south side and then go back and investigate.

The weather was good that day, and vision was unlimited. There were very few clouds, except one that clung to the peak, which was not unusual even on a nice day. Tomar called the forest rangers' office and was told that the trailer belonged to a professor. He was there on a grant to study the mountain and volcano. He had a permit, and his name was George Ohm. They even had a phone number for him.

Tomar had three others with him in the helicopter: Carol; Aiko, whom John promised would be involved with the investigation of the mountain; and her brother Hiroki. John was not there because Tomar insisted that he rest from his ordeal at the pier. Tomar knew the mountain better than any man, having lived in the area and climbed the mountain way before John Muir climbed Mount Rainier in 1888. He remembered the last significant eruption in 1820, a great one in 1854, and a smaller one in 1890. All of them caused great damage to the tribes of Native Americans and a few settlements of European people. Most of the eruption was ash and heat with a little lava flow that went off the east side at that time, but the rivers and low areas were filled with mud flows from the huge glaciers melting and flowing down the mountain. And he remembered the great one in his lifetime, about a thousand years ago, which caused major damage to the whole area up to fifty to sixty miles from the summit of the mountain.

Tomar respected nature and the natural volcanic activity of "the mountain." He had lived within the range of volcanoes in this area for a long time, but he could not shake the feeling that something unnatural was going on there.

"Tomar, what are we looking for?" asked Hiroki.

Tomar answered, "We are looking for anything unusual, like a trailer out in the middle of nowhere. Nacu just looked up who is sponsoring George Ohm's trip and investigation of the mountain, and it's Starr Corp out of Chicago, which is run by Jacob Starr, the CEO and main man in the world of profits. No way would he authorize this endeavor for the good of humankind. Profits and power are what he is about. We will set down about a half mile from the site in the clearing there and investigate on foot."

Carol asked Tomar, "Do you expect trouble?"

Tomar responded, "I expect to be ready if it comes. Remember, don't underestimate your opponent, and be ready for anything."

Aiko asked, "Do we know these people are opponents?"

Tomar replied, "We are working on suspicion only right now. What do you see with your gift of clairvoyance?"

Aiko closed her eyes and concentrated. After a few moments, she said, "I see trouble. I see the forest afire and devastation. It's like nothing survives."

"You answered your own question, Aiko. I will radio our position to Nacu when we set down."

They set down west of the camp area, and after they came to the clearing where the trailer was, Tomar said, "Please follow my lead. I will go in by myself to the trailer. Aiko, you come in from the south. Carol, you come in from the north side of the clearing. Hiroki, you circle around and come in from the east side of that location. You have twenty minutes to get into position before I approach the trailer. Please activate your earphones so you can all hear my conversation with whomever I meet. I will leave my device on voice-activated to transmit. Any questions?"

Hiroki said, "Yes, I can fly to the other side much faster."

Tomar answered, "No, we don't know what kind of tracking devices they may have. They may already know we are here; that is why I want you to come in from all sides. Only come to me if I signal or you see or hear that I need you. Your time starts right now. Set your watches."

As Tomar reached the trailer, the door suddenly opened, and Frances Mobley stepped out. He was much taller and larger than Tomar.

Frances asked, "Can I help you?"

Tomar answered, "I am Nathanial Tomar. I was hoping I could speak to Professor Ohm about the progress he has made in the study of the mountain. I am a fellow scientist of the Native American Institute of Northwest Studies and would be interested in discussing his findings."

"I'm sorry, sir. He is not here at the moment. Do you have a card or a way to contact you?"

"What is your name? Just what are you studying? And what knowledge about this do you have?" Tomar was searching for information.

"My name is Frances, and I help the professor with security and less technical matters. You must talk to him."

Just then, both men saw an SUV coming down the road into the clearing. It had a trail of dust behind it as it traveled toward the trailer.

Tomar asked, "Could this be the professor?"

Frances responded, "I think so."

They watched as the SUV pulled past the helicopter at the heliport and then came to a stop in front of the trailer. Jacob's driver was the first to get out. He walked over to the door to open it for the professor and Jacob Starr. The three of them walked up to the trailer, and Frances introduced Tomar to them. They all shook hands. When Jacob touched Tomar's hand, Tomar felt strength leave him and immediately pulled his hand away from Jacob's, trying not to draw any attention to his action.

Tomar asked, "Professor Ohm, just what can you tell me you find so interesting about the mountain?"

The professor responded, "Everything. It is one of nature's wonders and very active as volcanoes go. It is exciting to study one of the most powerful forces of nature there is."

Tomar then asked, "The activity has increased, according to the news recently. Can you share what your study tells you about the severity of the latest activity?"

Jacob interrupted the conversation. "Nathan Tomar, you are more than a scientist; you are the head of Tomar Industries Incorporated, one of the most admired privately owned companies in the United States. How you have kept your company from going public, I don't know."

Tomar answered, "And you are Jacob Starr, majority owner of Starr Corporation, one of the top fifty companies listed on the New York Stock Exchange. You are here to check up on Professor Ohm's progress on this mountain, which you are sponsoring, I presume. What do you expect to see, and what would bring a busy man like you to the great Northwest?"

Jacob smiled and replied, "We are here to test nature to see what makes the volcano tick, to find out the secrets it holds, and to check up on my investment, but you are here for more than just scientific curiosity, Mr. Tomar, aren't you?"

Tomar replied, "Jacob, you are a shrewd man who has not been known for an interest in nature unless it benefits you or your company personally."

Tomar was still fishing for information, trying to get Jacob to reveal the truth behind his visit. He was trying to evoke an emotional response from Jacob to see what he was capable of doing and his real intentions.

Jacob smiled as if he was amused by this conversation. "Mr. Tomar, I am sure I have no idea what you are talking about. Just why are you really here?"

Tomar answered, "I am here to get at the truth about this mountain and about you and your friends and what influence you have on the volcano."

Jacob raised his eyebrows and said, "Just what are you implying, Mr. Tomar? That we can have influence on a force of nature? You know how preposterous that sounds?"

Just then, Jacob's phone rang, and he excused himself and went into the trailer to talk. It was Trevor Donovan, head of the twenty-man security force that Jacob had called for from his office in Portland. They had arrived and spotted the other three of Tomar's band of visitors. He asked Jacob what he wanted them to do.

Jacob responded, "Watch them. If they move toward us, capture them. Only use deadly force if necessary."

Trevor acknowledged his orders and dispatched six men each to Carol and Aiko and then the rest to Hiroki.

When Jacob went into the trailer to talk to Trevor, the large SUV driver and Frances moved toward Tomar to make sure he did not leave until Jacob returned. They towered over him and outweighed him by several hundred pounds. Tomar looked up at them and said,

"That's okay, gentlemen; I am not going anywhere until I finish my conversation with your boss. I can deal with you later."

While this was going on, Carol had the trailer in sight at the end of the forest. She realized she was being watched by the movement of the animals; one raccoon and squirrel scurried away, and she felt from them the panic induced by strangers in their territory. As she was about to investigate, she heard the air move and instinctively reached up to catch a tranquilizer dart from a gun fired from the bushes. She whirled to throw the dart back in the direction it came from, released it, and hit the shooter in the arm. His body was soon overcome by the drugs in the dart, and he fell to the ground. Five other men came at her from different directions to subdue her physically. As the men reached about five feet away, Carol jumped straight up fourteen feet to the branch of a tree. Two of the men bumped heads as they leaped into the vacant area where she had been and fell to the ground. From her vantage point clinging to the branch, Carol fell on one of the other men and hit him with her feet in the solar plexus. He doubled over, and she knew he would not be in action for a while. Then she ducked as one man leaped at her. She reached toward his midsection to grab his military-type shirt and throw him at the other two guys left standing. They all fell at the foot of a large tree, wondering what had just hit them.

The other guys who had bumped heads recovered enough to lunge at her. Carol hit one man in the larynx, and the other, she side-kicked in the chest, knocking the wind from his lungs. As she was doing this, one of the three at the tree trunk recovered enough to unholster his handgun and aim it at her. He pulled the trigger and shot at her head, hoping he would end this quickly. Carol heard the firing pin hit the bullet in the gun and moved as fast as her reflexes would let her to turn her head just in time to feel the bullet graze her cheek and fly out into the forest. At this point, anger and adrenaline gave Carol the strength and speed to jump toward the man before he could let off another round, and she kicked him in the chest, sending him toward the large trunk of the tree. The force of the impact with the tree knocked the man out.

As the six men lay in the forest in different stages of consciousness, Carol used this opportunity to run into the forest at incredible speed, knowing it would be some time before the men could follow. She used the communication device to tell the others and Nacu what was going on in the trees, and they knew she was under attack.

At the Tomar Estate, John was at the cemetery and ancient burial grounds of Tomar's tribe. He was looking at a tombstone that said, "Mary Striker Tomar, Whose Love Was Greater than Her Life." The year on the stone was the date of John's birth. John had learned a lot recently about Mary and lamented he never knew her. Just then, he was struck by a sudden feeling that Tomar was in trouble.

At the same time, Nacu walked up and said, "Tomar's group is under attack. I heard a gunshot and report of an attack on Carol."

"Is she okay?"

"As far as I know, yes. She took out six men. The others are unaccounted for."

John pointed back at the mansion and said, "Please get Phillip and Samuel and send them to the hangar bay. Is the *Lightning* ready?"

Nacu nodded his head up and down. "Yes. I will get the others, and the craft is fueled and ready to go, no missiles but the cannons are fully armed." The hangar bay was next to the exercise room area on the Tomar Estate, which was built right into the mountain with a movable camouflaged roof that one could not see from the air when it was closed.

Jacob walked out of the trailer and said to Frances and the driver, "Take hold of Tomar." The men grabbed Tomar by the arms and held him, and then Jacob said, "Tomar, you need to tell me what your companions and you are doing here right now, or these men will hurt you."

Tomar looked right into Jacob's eyes and said, "I heard the gunshots in the trees. You'd better not hurt anyone, or you will regret it." Tomar knew Carol was all right from her transmission, which he heard through his earpiece, but he was not sure of the others.

Jacob shook his head from side to side and said, "You aren't exactly in a position of strength right now. You need to talk, or these men will rip your arms off."

The pressure they were putting on his shoulders was enormous. Tomar believed they had the power to do exactly what Jacob suggested. He wanted to get more information from Jacob—if his shoulders could take the pressure these giants were exerting on them—so he replied, "Jacob, let me tell you what I see here. You tell me if I'm wrong. You are a person of considerable financial and political power, and you also possess great physical and mental powers. You have put together this project on the mountain to tap into the power of this volcano using the expertise of Professor Ohm, and you have in your employ genetically enhanced goons like Tweedle Dum and Tweedle Dee here to do the heavy work. Oh yes, you have at your disposal hundreds of trained military to do your bidding."

Jacob was not amused by Tomar's rant. He looked angry. He told Frances, "Take Tomar behind the trailer. Take each arm, and make a wish, and dispose of the body down the shaft in the mountain."

Just then, Jacob's phone rang; he went into the trailer with the professor to answer. It was Trevor Donovan again. He sounded very upset when he said, "I have ten men injured and three men unconscious of the twenty men. Why didn't you tell me we were dealing with meta-humans? I have a man who burned five men with flames from his hands and a woman with the strength of a bear and the speed of a cheetah who took out six men. Not to mention a woman who cut the net we trapped her in with a samurai sword and then somehow disabled six of my men. The man melted the bullets we shot at him. I have called for reinforcements, but that will take three hours or more."

Jacob was already reaching out mentally to see where the metahumans were. He said to Trevor, "Double the force you asked for. I want a hundred men here in three hours to protect the project. And bring what men you have to the trailer with any heavy firepower to protect the trailer." Trevor acknowledged what he said and hung up.

Professor Ohm heard the conversation and said, "We can control the operation from the site of the shaft. I have a minisite there, which we can use if the trailer is compromised. How soon can you get the bomb here?"

Jacob answered, "The bomb is six hours away in transit. Can you blow the mountain in forty-eight hours?"

"Yes, I can. It's not an exact science, but I will start it now while the trailer is still operational and finish remotely at the shaft site for the bomb if necessary."

Jacob instructed the professor to start the process. Then Jacob concentrated and sent a delusional mental suggestion to Hiroki that his sister and Carol were military men trying to shoot him and take his sister captive. Jacob suggested to Hiroki that he burn them.

Tomar was in the back of the trailer with Frances and Jacob's driver and bodyguard about to be pulled apart by the arms. As the men started to pull harder, Tomar's arms faded through their hands, and Tomar was free. The arms solidified again, and then Tomar hit the jaw of Jacob's driver with the force of a sledgehammer and knocked him against the trailer. As he did this, he back-kicked the rear of Frances's knee and took his legs out from under him. While Frances was on his knees, he hit the back of his head with the same force he had applied to his partner. To his amazement, both men were stunned but not out. He took this opportunity and ran to the south end of the trailer to see what had happened to the others. It was starting to get dark, and he could see flashes of light in the forest. As he got closer, he could see it was Hiroki throwing flames at his sister and Carol, who were crouched behind a large tree to keep him from burning them. The tree bark was scorched, and Hiroki was yelling at Carol and Aiko, "Return my sister, or I will burn you!"

Carol and Aiko were trying to reason with him, but all he heard from them was, "We have your sister; give yourself up, or we will kill her."

Tomar could see an aura of heat around Hiroki's body that protected him from bullets and projectiles. Tomar was not seen by anyone yet so he picked up a hand-sized rock that would survive the heat zone around him and threw it. It hit him in the back. The shock of the rock knocked him down and broke the mental suggestion sent by Jacob. Hiroki shook himself on the ground and said, "What hit me?"

Aiko ran to his side. The air around him was still warm, but she held her brother and said, "Are you okay?"

As Aiko cradled Hiroki, he said, "Sister, I think I have a broken rib; it really hurts."

Tomar had joined them by this time and said to Hiroki, "Are you able to walk? We need to get to the helicopter."

All four of the group heard John over the receiver in their ears. He was transmitting from a jet aircraft. He said, "This is John. I am two minutes away. What is the status? Are all people accounted for?"

Tomar answered, "John, we are all here on the south side of the trailer in the trees. I want you to cover us as we try to get back to the helicopter in a clearing west of the trailer. Also, I want you to fire at the trailer when you know it is clear of people. Damage it beyond repair by missile or guns. When you get a chance, connect with me for further instructions."

John responded, "Copy that. I can see the trailer firing some warning shots right now. We'll make a run on the west side of the clearing in a moment."

Tomar could hear the jet engine and the guns firing and see the flash of the guns through the trees. Hiroki painfully got up, and they moved toward the helicopter.

Carol and Tomar helped Hiroki. It was painful at first, but he could walk at a normal pace, and he was getting better by the minute. Carol asked Tomar, "You have a jet fighter?"

They were moving as fast as they could toward the helicopter.

Tomar answered, "Yes, I had it made two years ago. It is a copy of the F-35B supersonic jet, which can hover in the air and fly Mach 3. It has a stealth design so radar has a hard time locating it. It also seats four people by design."

Carol remarked, "You never cease to amaze me, Tomar."

At the trailer, the professor was still trying to set things up to blow the mountain. Jacob grabbed his cell phone and called Trevor again.

"Do you still have the Russian SAMs in your arsenal? You must protect the trailer! We have to finish what we are doing!"

"I have two about fifty feet from me. I will fire one myself at the jet."

Jacob approved and told the professor to continue. Professor Ohm was uneasy with the shots from the jet overhead, but he continued the procedure to cause an eruption of the mountain.

John made his last run on the west side of the clearing to secure Tomar and his group passage to the helicopter, and then he put the jet in hover mode four hundred yards in front of the trailer and on the loudspeaker said, "Clear the trailer or be destroyed with it. You have thirty seconds before I fire."

As John slowly glided closer to the trailer, in the dim light, he saw a man outside the trailer staring at the jet in defiance of what he had said. Phillip was with him in the cab and so was Samuel, although he would rather have been on the ground.

Phillip said through his oxygen mask microphone, "What is that fool doing? Just standing there waiting to die?"

John tried to connect mentally with the man and to his surprise found himself in excruciating pain and the mental battle of his life. Thoughts of failure and a numbness came over his body. He was frozen physically and could not move.

Phillip, who was a pilot himself, felt the jet lunge and grabbed the control wheel in front of him. He said to John, "What's wrong, John? Pull yourself together! Let me have the controls."

John began fighting back mentally and slowly came to his senses, but just then, Samuel and Phillip saw a fast-moving blimp coming toward them on the radar screen.

Phillip yelled, "Missile!"

John gave the controls over to Phillip, but there was no time for him to maneuver out of the way of the land-to-air missile sent by Trevor on the north side of the clearing. With only seconds before the collision of missile and aircraft, John broke Jacob's mental hold and sent a large rock on the ground toward Jacob with enough kinetic energy to knock him off his feet and break any future mental holds. At the same time, he formed a force field around the jet to protect the aircraft from the collision of the missile.

The explosion was spectacular. Trevor, who shot the missile, and Jacob, who was on his knees from the rock that had knocked him down, were both convinced that they had stopped the threat. However, when the fire and smoke cleared, the jet remained.

In the cockpit, Samuel and Phillip were shocked. They thought they would die in the explosion. They looked at John to see how he was. John looked and felt exhausted. He said to Phillip, "Go back to the mansion base. There is another missile, and I don't think I have enough strength to stop this one."

Phillip grabbed the control and changed from the hover mode to fly. They headed back to their mountain home. Tomar was in contact with Phillip after he saw the explosion. He had already started the helicopter, and they were headed home also. Tomar said, "What happened? Are you okay?"

Phillip answered, "We are okay, thanks to John. There is another threat. We are leaving the area. We'll inform you of details when we meet."

Tomar acknowledged what he had said and headed home. John closed his eyes and said nothing all the way back.

Chapter 9

Jane had been at the jail during the afternoon and interviewed Jack Nash. She was discussing what Jack had said with Mike Morris in the Twilight Bar and Restaurant. It was near the downtown area of Seattle. Jane had asked Mike to discuss the possible identity of the third person in her fateful meeting with Nash. They were at a table near the window and had just ordered. It was a beautiful night, and Mike was wondering to himself if there was any chance Jane was romantically interested in him when Jane said, "Are you listening to me, Mike? I was talking about my visit with Jack Nash today. He said the other man's name was John, and he was very sorry he stabbed me and blamed it on a demonic entity who possessed him."

"Sorry, Ms. Watkins, I was distracted. I had a busy day at work. I want to thank you for dinner. As far as what I know about the other guy at the place you met Nash, his voice is clearly on the recording; it's very weak at times, but the voice is there until the recording was turned off or ran out of tape."

Jane reached into her purse and pulled out the picture someone had taken at the pier with the explosion over the water and asked Mike, "Can you do anything with this picture to get an identification of the man in this camera shot?"

She handed the picture to Mike. He looked at it for a moment and said, "Honestly, this four-by-six picture does not tell me much. Do you have the original digital source or negative?"

Jane looked disappointed and said, "No, Mike, I got it from someone in the crowd at the pier. They took a picture of someone flying in the air just before the explosion over the water. They sent it to my phone by text message, and I printed it out later."

Mike's eyes widened, and he chuckled. "Then you have a digital picture on your phone?"

"Wow, I guess I do. How do I give it to you?"

Mike smiled and said, "Send it to two-oh-six-nine-five-seven-two-three-four-three, and I will have it."

Jane felt dumb and, as she reached in her purse to get her phone, said, "I'm sorry, Mike, me and electronic devices don't get along too well. I found it in my text and am sending it to your number right now."

Mike pulled his iPad tablet out of his briefcase and heard the beep of a text coming to his tablet. He found the picture and put it into his photos. He took a look at it and then magnified the pixels as far out as he could. He could see that there was a blurred face of a blond man wearing a hooded coat with something in his hands. He used a picture enhancer to clear the picture, and it helped some. Then he gave Jane the enhanced picture and asked her, "Is that your man?"

Jane could not wait to look. She grabbed the tablet and studied the enhanced picture close up. "I only got a glimpse of him before he put himself behind glowing armor to block his features. Can you see what color eyes he has? He had the most beautiful blue eyes I have ever seen."

Mike could see that she had a strong emotional bond to her savior. He felt disappointed. Perhaps he realized that there could be no chance for him with her, and friendship was all they would ever have. However, he encouraged Jane, "Maybe with more study on my computer at home, I can find out what color his eyes are or some other identifying marks in the picture. Give me some time to study it more."

The salad had just arrived; Jane took a drink of the red wine in her glass and said, "Thanks, Mike. You're a good friend. Please don't say anything to the people at the *Gazette*. I just know it's him. Now, I have a detective to see. Enjoy your dinner, Mike. You earned it."

Mike smiled and looked down at his salad.

Two hours had passed since the intrusion of Tomar and his friends near the trailer. Jacob looked deep in thought, and he seemed shaken by his mental ordeal with the pilot of the jet aircraft. He did not have much success in the psychic interchange but did link with the fire thrower in his mind. He also got much information from Trevor about the abilities of the meta-beings who had invaded the project, and more men were arriving from Portland. The forest rangers in the area came by and wanted answers about the noise of an explosion, the scorched earth they saw when they arrived, and the report of gunfire. Jacob convinced them through his mental powers that the reports were false and there was no gunfire or burned earth. After they left, he closed his eyes and seemed to be in meditation. He used his power to go out mentally and change the perception of anyone in the area.

After the forest rangers left, Trevor said to Jacob, "Boss, do you expect the meta-humans back soon? It will be another forty-five minutes to an hour before all the men you requested are here."

"I think they will lick their wounds, but they will come back as soon as they can. Set up a perimeter around the clearing. I want nothing to get through. And send ten men to the remote location where the shaft is. In a few hours, a truck will be arriving with a very precious cargo. It must be protected at all cost."

Professor Ohm was proceeding as planned. In another four hours, he would go to stage 2 of the procedure to blow the top off the mountain. It was slower than the demonstration to Jacob because he had to build the pressure very slowly to maximize the explosion with the bomb.

Jacob walked into the trailer and asked the professor, "Are we on schedule? Will it happen as you planned?"

"Yes, the numbers and pressures are where I would expect them. I will start phase 2 soon. One more stage or phase here at the trailer, and then the last two stages will be at the remote location where the shaft is. That is the critical part."

"What is the point of no return? When do we evacuate the area?"

Professor Ohm replied, "At the forty-fifth hour of operation, which gives us about forty-three hours from now."

"Can it be done any faster?"

"Not if you want a big explosion and lots of damage. The heavy lava has to be in the correct place with the right pressure behind it so when the bomb goes off, it is like the last straw of activity blowing the top right off the mountain toward the populated areas. There won't even be a lot of earthquakes until the last moment; therefore, it will catch people by surprise."

Jacob suggested, "What about a plan B if that does not work because of interference."

"Anything less than forty-five hours will result in a lot less damage and devastation. You must understand what I am doing has never been done before. All the math and model runs have been calling for forty-eight hours. Can you and your men give me that?"

Jacob remembered the conversation he had had with Madam Scarlet La Brasa and how she had said, "Jacob Starr, you are a remarkable man. You have never been truly challenged in what you seek, but I saw in your eyes that the day is approaching when you will be shaken to your very soul." Then he was struck by something he had never experienced before—doubt. He looked at the professor and said, "You will have the forty-eight hours you need, Professor Ohm."

There was a bright light and then the shadow figure of a woman. As the light dimmed, the figure took a form. She was a beautiful woman with blonde hair, blue eyes, and a big smile. She looked down at the baby bundle in her arms and said, "Momma loves you, and everything is going to be all right." Then the woman began to sing.

> There are stars in the sky that sparkle bright,
> And the sun it breaks every morn',
> But you lit up my life, gave me joy,
> And delight the day that you were born.
> Sleep well, my beloved, and dream sweet dreams,
> For life is yours to explore,
> There is no limit; you will do great things,
> But remember this I implore,
> That a mother's love follows you to the end,
> And I have loved you from the start.
> For we don't just live for us every day,
> But for others till the day we depart.
> Remember, you are loved, you are loved,
> And everything is going to be all right,
> Because love is the answer to sustain all things.
> Study love with all your might.
> Remember, you are loved, you are loved,
> And everything is going to be all right,
> Remember, you are loved, you are loved,
> And everything is going to be all right.

Then the woman faded, and there was a tombstone with words that were seen before: "Mary Striker Tomar, Whose Love Was Greater than Her Life." With that, John woke up from his dream in tears. He got up slowly from his bed and walked over to the bathroom where he washed his face. Sleep had claimed him since he came back from the mountain. The ordeal had left him exhausted, but after several hours of sleep, he was feeling better and went to find Tomar and the others.

John went to the kitchen first to get some refreshment and found Nacu preparing something to eat.

Nacu looked at John and said, "How are you feeling, John? Can I fix you something to eat?"

John looked at Nacu and replied, "I am not hungry, but I am thirsty. Do we have any juice? I am feeling better."

Nacu pointed at the refrigerator and said, "Yes, it is in there. Let me get it for you."

With that, John sat down at the bar stool and looked at Nacu again. As he leaned against the serving bar, he said, "I got my lunch handed to me. We barely got out of there alive. I am not too sure I want to face that telepath again. He is very powerful. Made me lose control. It took all I had to snap out of it."

Nacu handed John his drink and replied, "Yes, but you snapped out of it in time to keep the others with you from perishing in an explosion. That took great mental discipline. And he won't catch you by surprise again like that."

John looked down at the glass of juice and said, "All I could think was to protect my thoughts and mind from invasion, and in that, I am sure I was successful. The by-product of doing that is I know a lot about him and what their plans are. He did not block his inner thoughts or intentions. He wants to rule the world through deceit and mind control. He also wants to control nature and believes he has the resources to do just that."

Just then, the professor and Tomar walked into the kitchen. Tomar was the first to speak.

"John, how are you feeling? Albert and I were coming to see how you are doing. You were pretty wiped out when you came from the mission to the mountain. I know you were instrumental in keeping the team on the aircraft alive."

John answered, "Yes, after the mental attack on me in the aircraft, I did not have much power left, so I put all I had in reserves to protect the *Lightning* from destruction. I was spent after that. However, I feel much better now. I am having some juice and am almost back to normal."

Nacu smiled and said, "Yes, whatever normal is for you."

Albert laughed, and Tomar smiled also. They both sat down on empty bar stools. Then Albert asked John, "Can you tell us what happened in the jet and how you were attacked?"

John nodded and then said, "I was about to fire some warning shots over the trailer when I found myself paralyzed. I could not move, and I realized it was a mental attack bent on grounding or crashing the plane. It was intense, the strongest I have ever experienced in the mind. I was in the battle of my life. Finally, I used my power and threw a rock at the man in front of the trailer. Hit him in the chest, and that helped me break free enough to recover and block the missile heading toward the jet. The mental exchange between us caught me by surprise. I was not expecting a telepath with enormous powers on the site. All I could think was to defend my thoughts and identity from attack. I am sure I was successful in that, but the man must have not realized my powers and left himself open to me. For thirty seconds, which seemed like an eternity, I saw a man with great plans that included ruling the world and controlling nature itself, namely the volcano at Mount Rainier."

Tomar agreed with John by saying, "I challenged the man you saw in front of the trailer with that very idea of controlling the mountain. His name is Jacob Starr, and he is a power-hungry man of business and ruthless in his dealings with everyone who comes against him. There was a Professor Ohm there also, who gave him the technical knowledge to think it was possible. Jacob interrupted my interview with the professor and took away my chance to find out more. I was under mental attack the whole time I was at the trailer and had to block him. He also sent a delusional mental control to Hiroki that his sister was caught by the military men, and he almost burned his sister and Carol."

Professor Albert Hughes shook his head side to side and said, "This is crazy to think a man could control a force of nature like a volcano. Do you have any idea how many metric tons the mountain weighs and how impossible it would be to make it erupt?"

Nathan Tomar followed that by saying, "Albert, you must quit thinking of what is impossible and think of what is possible. You of all people know what it takes in nature to cause an eruption of a volcano. What would a man have to do if he could to make the volcano erupt? How would he do it?"

Albert smiled and said, "I have seen a lot of things I thought were impossible in the past weeks that made me think out of the scientific box of probability. To make that possible, someone would have to change the flow of lava under the mountain. He would have to stack the heavier lava in such a place to build the pressure to an enormous amount to displace earth and rock and ice to make its way to the top of the mountain and erupt. Nature takes time in doing that, and most volcanic eruptions are preceded by much seismic activity or many earthquakes.

"While there is no set way of eruption in the Northwest, many volcano eruptions have blown the top right off the mountain because of the heavy lava found in this area, like with Mount Saint Helens. It might be possible if someone could set up a ten-mile radius grid of the mountain with control points that somehow changed the makeup of rock and earth and lava under the ground to build the pressure. This eventually would cause an eruption of some degree, but I can't tell you without doing some calculations against the mass and weight of the earth and ice on and under the surface of the mountain. Also, most explosive eruptions have an event moment when something causes the volcano to blow the top right off the mountain."

John listened to what the professor had to say and then said out loud, "They have a nuclear bomb."

Everyone looked in astonishment at John.

Tomar said, "They have *what*?"

103

John looked back at Tomar and said again, "They have a nuke. Could that cause your event if the pressure was just right?"

They all looked right at the professor. He replied, "Well, yes, I guess if the pressure was just right, and I don't think it would have to be more than a megaton, but I would have to do some calculations. How do you know that, John?"

John answered, "In that moment of attack at the trailer site, the man you called Jacob left his mind open to me, and I saw he had a nuclear device in transit to his location. At the time of the conflict, it was about six hours away. According to the clock, that means it is almost there by now."

Tomar looked at Nacu and asked him, "Do you still have those military drones we got awhile ago? Are they operational?"

Nacu nodded and said, "We have a handheld that has a five-mile range and one-hour flight time and one with a twenty-mile range that can stay in the air for about two hours. They are very quiet in the stealth mode."

Tomar instructed, "Nacu, you and Phillip work covertly and place the smaller one on the trailer and the larger one in a tree overlooking the clearing where the trailer is after it makes a circle of the area. And do your best not to be spotted by anyone."

Nacu acknowledged what was said and went to find Phillip. Tomar looked at John and Professor Hughes and said, "Now, John, can you tell us more about what you know from your encounter with Jacob?"

They talked more about the incident.

"I am sorry; Detective Jones is interviewing a suspect at the moment, and he may be some time. Can I help you?"

Jane had almost made it to Jones's desk in the Seattle Homicide Department. She was still in her dinner clothes from the time she spent with Mike. Someone with a badge, Sergeant Jackson, stopped her and inquired why she was there. Jane was restless after dinner and came by the police department to talk to Jones about the third man at the crime scene, where she had been stabbed to see if he knew more about it now. She answered the sergeant, "I am Jane Watkins and was stabbed by Jack Nash, the Slasher suspect. I heard at the front Detective Jones was here, and I wanted to talk to him about the incident."

Sergeant Jackson was a large man in a blue Seattle police uniform. He looked at Jane and then said, "Is this important? He is pretty busy right now. Can I take a message, and he can make contact with you later?"

Jane wanted to see him tonight if possible and said, "Sergeant Jackson, I would really like to see him now, if you please. I am having a hard time with what happened and would like to talk to Detective Jones about it."

The sergeant looked sympathetic and said, "We have the chaplain available if you like. Maybe he can help."

Jane looked right at him and said, "No, I just have to settle in my mind some things about the attack. It will help me sleep tonight to get the answers."

"I will tell Jones you're here. There is a chair you may sit in right there."

Jane sat down in the chair. It was very close to Jones's desk. She could see two pictures on the desk. One was of a young, dark-haired, very pretty woman, whom she assumed was his girlfriend or wife, and the other was Jones with his arm around a blond-haired, blue-eyed man about the same age. The background looked familiar, like a university, possibly the University of Washington in Seattle. Just then, Detective Jones walked toward the desk. He was in a casual shirt with blue jeans. He looked tired, but he was polite when he said, "I understand you wanted to talk to me, Ms. Watkins?"

Jane was startled and answered, "Why, yes, Detective Jones. I am still very troubled by a few things in the investigation of Nash. I remember a third man there who saved me from the attack by Nash.

I need to know if your investigation uncovered that fact also and if you are looking for that man. I have a hard time sleeping at night, thinking I hallucinated the whole thing."

He stood by his desk, looked her in the eyes, and said, "I must admit when I saw you that night and again the next day, I had a hard time understanding your story—that is, how you could be stabbed and have no evidence of a wound, although there was plenty blood, so I interviewed the paramedics and the doctor in the ER at the hospital, and both found evidence of head trauma from when he slammed you to the ground. There was also a small amount of blood in your nose, which could explain the blood on your dress. It could have come from a severe nosebleed. However, that does not explain why Jack Nash did not finish the job with the knife that we found on the scene. So there is a possibility that there was a third man there to stop Jack from ending your life.

"That is why I asked to hear the tape of the incident that you brought to the office. It shows a conversation with Nash with a lot of crazy talk and then the bump of the purse hitting the ground and muffled sounds. There is one voice that could have been someone else there, but it is so muffled by your purse, it is hard to identify, much less use in a search for him. I am sorry; that's the best that I can do to help you sleep tonight. Even so, that is where we are at in the investigation. There is still plenty more evidence to link him to the other attacks and deaths. This is probably more than I should tell you at this time, so don't try to print any of this right now until the trial, please. I just wanted to help you out personally."

Jane could see he was good at interviewing people. He kept everything under control at all times. He also did not tell the whole truth. The tape she had given him was the original. Mike Morris had made copies of the tape, and it clearly indicated someone with a different voice there after the attack. One couldn't quite make out what he said, but there was someone else there; she had heard it. So she changed her strategy and said, "Thank you so much, Detective Jones, for accepting the possibility there was someone else there. I will not print any of our conversations. I will let you go back to your work, but before you leave, I could not help noticing the picture of the beautiful woman on your desk. Is she your wife?"

Jones smiled and said, "No, she is my girlfriend, Amanda; she is finishing her degree at university before we get married—if I can convince her to marry me."

Jane remarked, "She is lovely, and the guy in the other picture with you, who is he?"

Jones looked surprised and dropped the smile from his face. He looked at the picture and said, "That is a good friend from college named John. We graduated together six years ago."

Just then, Sergeant Jackson came close and said to Jones, "They need you in the interrogation room, Detective Jones; it's important."

"I will be right there." He looked at Jane and said, "Ms. Watkins, if you will excuse me."

Jane was disappointed. She wanted more information on the guy named John in the picture, but she was interrupted so she smiled and said, "Detective Jones, thanks for talking to me."

Jones nodded at Jane and left the office. Jane could not take her eyes off the man in the picture next to Jones. She had to find out more about him. Jane thought, *If Jones is not going to tell me more, perhaps the university graduating class list from six years earlier will give me a clue. I might need Mike Morris's help with this.* After another look at the picture, she left the office to go home.

Chapter 10

Phillip and Nacu had arrived near the clearing with the trailer on Mount Rainier by helicopter, but had to land several miles from the site so they would not be detected. They moved closer to the trailer and then launched the drones. The smaller drone had just enough battery life to make it to the trailer, but the backup battery for the camera could operate for about thirty-four hours. The small helicopter landed on the trailer, and Nacu directed the camera toward the opening. The larger drone was about three feet long with four multiple blades and could stay in the air for about 120 minutes. Nacu made a circle of the clearing at five hundred feet. In stealth mode, it made very little noise.

With the infrared camera, they could see there were many men around the clearing and much activity at the trailer. In the clearing were parked several large vans and SUVs. There were also five Hummers and three pickups. It looked like they had enough men and equipment to wage a small war. The lights were still on at the trailer, and the heat signatures showed four men in there. The battery life of the drone was below 40 percent, and there was no place that Nacu could find to land the larger drone, so he directed it back to their location. One of the men in the clearing thought he heard a strange humming sound coming from the air above him but lost track of the sound when a truck drove up to the trailer and covered up any noise. It was just before dawn, and Phillip and Nacu had successfully completed Tomar's request. They arrived back at the Tomar Estate to share the information with the others.

Tomar was asleep in the chapel, lying on the ground, but was awakened by the sound of the helicopter arriving back to the hangar bay. He had come there to pray after his interview with John about what he had found out from Jacob and the others at Mount Rainier. He learned that these men on the mountain really believed they could cause an exploding eruption of the mountain that would destroy life and property in most of the area and then blame it on a natural event. He was troubled by the destruction of life, both human and nature. Would he have to kill to stop these men? He was asking God in prayer to show him a way to save lives, both in the area and at the site.

John walked into the chapel and looked troubled. He had also been awakened by the arrival of the helicopter. He talked to Tomar, "Tomar, I need to talk to you about what we are walking into with Jacob on the mountain. Should we contact the authorities? It is a lot of responsibility to take on by ourselves."

Tomar smiled at John and said, "First, I want to know how you are doing and feeling, Son?"

"I am back to being me. I feel very well. I learned a lot from my first encounter with Jacob, and he won't have me at a disadvantage again when we meet."

"That's the spirit, John. I should have warned you about him. There just wasn't time; everything happened so fast. In answer to your question about the authorities, who has enough influence to help us? Who would believe us? And who can we trust?"

John looked down and then right at Tomar and said, "I would trust Detective John Jones of the Seattle Police with my life, and General Wade Eiling from McChord Air Force Base has helped us in the past."

"Yes, they are two important people we know and are very trustworthy, but do we know if Jacob can do what they are planning to do?"

John thought for a second and said, "Well, they believe they can, and I know they were responsible for the blow off on the mountain a couple of days ago. Professor Ohm did that to prove to Jacob that he had control of the mountain."

Tomar listened to John and remarked, "Put the question of contacting the authorities aside for the moment. Is the group of young people ready for the conflict with Jacob? It could cost them their lives. They did well last time, but I have reservations about getting them involved. We still know very little about the extent of their power and resources."

"Why did you put these people together at this time if it was not for something like this? Plus, I don't think you and I alone can stop what is going on there. We need help. The wiser we are, the fewer lives will be at stake, and you know we have to do this."

Tomar looked back at John and said, "I was led to put this gathering of special people together for the end-time crisis that will arrive. It was foretold that there would be a falling away first, and then people's hearts would wax cold and lead to the acceptance of great evil that would rule the world. It would be started by a great world leader. Perhaps his day will come but not today, as long as there is life in us. We will postpone the triumph of evil on this day and save as many people as we can."

"Nice speech, Smoha … I mean Tomar." The voice came from the corner of the chapel. Neither John nor Tomar had heard him enter the dwelling. Just then, the man stepped toward John and Tomar and continued, "One thing you forget, that the great evil will not triumph until I and my earthly companion die, and I am not dead yet. I still am the Traveler. My duty right now is to keep a record of important events as they happen concerning eternal things. You are here to turn the tide of evil and stop the premature advance of one man. It is not his time to rule, even though he thinks he is the one."

Tomar smiled and said, "Enoch! Eli said you were in the area. Only you and he can make an appearance with no noise. You have to show me that trick sometime. I like your modern clothes. The shirt and pants look good on you."

Enoch wore a pair of blue jeans and a dark-gray shirt with a light overcoat but still had sandals on his feet. He had a full beard but shorter hair. He smiled and said, "Yes, Elias thought I could dress more like the rest of the world, but I refused to cut off the beard."

Tomar looked at John and said, "John, this is Enoch, the Traveler. I don't know where he sleeps, but I do see him when I am involved in an event worth recording. I guess that is the conflict on the mountain. You wouldn't tell me how it comes out, would you, Enoch?"

Enoch smiled and said, "You know I just record the events and do not know the outcome, but I do know you and have full confidence in you and your abilities. Tomar, may I remind you that volcanoes are not only access to the melting fire of the earth, but there are gateways to the spiritual underworld there also. The one of power on the mountain may be able to see or sense them."

Tomar looked surprised and said, "Enoch, you know I am aware of that. It hasn't slipped my mind. What would Jacob do with the access to the underworld? He must be in league with the demonic forces. That is how I believe, with selective breeding, he and his men exhibit extraordinary powers and abilities. Access to the forces there would give him great power, but this is knowledge that the powers of evil already have, I am sure. You and Eli always present me with mysteries when I see you."

John was listening to the conversation and remarked to his father, "Tomar, there is a lot about the spirit world you haven't told me. That means that there are dimensional-temporal distortions between worlds there. They may be visible to the right pair of eyes. I will look for them next time I go to the mountain. When are we going, Tomar?"

Tomar looked at Enoch and then John and said, "I have a plan to minimize the loss of life and succeed in dismantling their effort to cause the mountain to erupt. Have everyone meet in the hall at 0700 hours, and we will discuss the plan there."

"It was six to one. We should have been able to subdue her easily, but she kicked our asses, dodged a bullet aimed at her head, and ran into the forest faster than anyone I have ever seen. The other smaller woman, according to Darrel in the other group, cut her way out of the net they threw over her with some samurai sword and then, with a wave of her hand, held six men down with an invisible force while she ran away. Not to mention the five men that a guy with flames shooting out from his hands torched. This is not what I signed on for." A man named Joe, one of those Carol had thrown against the tree, was telling his story to a new man named Bob from Portland.

Bob had arrived at the camp near the trailer the previous night, and he responded, "And the two big bodyguards of the professor and Jacob, who are as large as bears, got their bells rung pretty good by one guy behind the trailer, I heard. What the hell is going on here anyway? Plus, someone said there was an explosion in front of the trailer last night."

Joe then said, "Yes, there was a jet hovering in front of the trailer. Trevor fired a Russian SAM at the aircraft, and there was an explosion, but the jet survived and flew off. It was crazy! I would not believe it if I hadn't seen it. The jet was not even scratched. These people are superhuman and no telling what they are capable of. But the pay is good, and Jacob is no one to mess with himself. Saw him take down five guys in combat training. His 'free-form' fighting is like none I have ever seen, and he can mess with your head and drain any strength you have. And Professor Ohm, I swear I have seen lightning come from his hands. Some think it is how he got the power to bore the hole into the earth at the other location up the mountain."

Bob replied, "Well, there are a lot of things I don't understand, but this I know: I don't want to piss off the boss. Some guys who did that, or questioned his orders, have never been seen again, and I don't think they retired."

Just then, Trevor came over the communication device on their shoulders and said there would be a meeting in the clearing near the trailer. All hands were required to be there in twenty minutes.

Joe and Bob looked at each other, and Bob said, "Well, this is where we get the official bullcrap about what we are doing here. I don't think that pay is going to be enough for this."

Joe picked up his gun and bag and replied, "You got that right."

Nacu was recording Trevor's conversation with his men in front of the trailer with the camera on the small drone on top of the roof. Trevor had a very loud voice, so he did not have to turn the volume up very much. Trevor designated twenty men in group orange and red to escort the truck that had arrived the previous night to the remote location up the mountain for the professor to use there. He told them it was important that it arrive there safely and they were to stand guard until the professor could examine the contents of the truck further and install the equipment at that site.

Group orange and red would leave in sixty minutes to deliver the truck to the other place up the mountain. Trevor did not give them a time period for the arrival of the professor. The rest of the men would guard the trailer from any interference until the brain trust, namely Professor Ohm and Jacob, moved to the other location. He also told them to check the transport vehicles to make sure they were in good working order because they might have to evacuate the area quickly in the next twenty-four hours.

It looked like the men were well-armed, and Jacob ended the talk by saying, "What we are doing here is important to Starr Enterprises, and employees who follow instructions will receive a big bonus.

If we are successful with this operation, it will bring worldwide attention to the goals of the company and promote a way of life that will benefit all mankind. I will not tolerate insubordination but will reward those who follow instructions. Because of the importance of the operation, deadly force is authorized. No one can be allowed to stop us. You answer directly to your group leader and Trevor, and they answer to me."

Everyone looked confident and listened intently to Jacob. They seemed to be in a heightened emotional state. It was possible Jacob was using his mental powers to induce a state of euphoria and confidence in what they were doing. Trevor finished by saying, "Check your equipment and communication devices, and do what your group leader tells you. All group leaders follow the instructions we discussed. If you have questions about your assignments, meet with me now. Otherwise, move out."

With that, Nacu joined the others who were talking in the library of the mansion. He interrupted John and told the group what was going on at the site on Mount Rainier.

Tomar looked at Phillip and asked him, "Phillip, can you make it to their campsite and place a GPS tracker where that truck is going so we know where the other location is and can meet you there later? I want you to do it on foot. We can't risk being seen in a helicopter or plane."

Phillip looked at Tomar and said, "Sure, I can run the whole distance if you want, and I am positive it will eliminate detection that way. I got some rest and refreshments, so I am ready to go."

Tomar then said, "Nacu will give you the tracker and show you on the map the straightest route with the fewest obstacles for the run. I want you to leave in a few minutes, but before you go, Albert has something to show all of you."

The professor reached down, picked up a cardboard box, and placed it on the table in the room. He pulled out several masks that looked like they were made of rubber or elastic. The masks covered the head and forehead but had an opening in the front for the nose and eyes. The mouth and jaw was open also. He said, "Each one of you has one to wear over your head. I tried to match the color of the jumpsuit you usually wear. It must cover your cranium to do you any good."

He then started to throw them to the appropriate people. He threw a yellow-green one to Phillip.

Phillip said, "You are giving me a mask so I don't mess my hair up?"

Albert smiled and said, "Well, I did not make them to make you look good or keep your hair straight. They are designed to prevent a mental attack and make you invisible to Jacob, so he can't sense you, only see you. Here, let me demonstrate."

The professor put an extra gray one over his head, and then he asked John to tell him what he had for breakfast.

John looked at him, laughed, and said, "Well, you had a poached egg and wheat toast with coffee, black, and then a glass of orange juice."

The professor looked disappointed and said, "You know that is not how we tested it earlier. How is it you can read my thoughts now?"

John smiled and replied, "Professor, that's what you have every morning. You are a real creature of habit. I was just messing with you. Except for hearing your heartbeat and seeing you stand there, I don't perceive you with my mental abilities at all."

Albert smiled and said, "You Yanks are always having fun. Now please, John, reach out and touch me. Tell me what my wife liked to do in her spare time. I know you have no preknowledge of that."

John reached out, touched the professor on the shoulder, and then said, "She liked to sew, knit, and work with needlepoint while you worked and would watch you when you came home while she worked on a flowered tapestry she never finished."

Professor Albert Hughes's eyes began to water. He hesitated for a moment, and then he looked around the group of wannabe heroes and cleared his throat. "Thank you, John, for the demonstration showing that if Jacob has physical contact with your person, he can have access to your mind, and as Tomar found out, he can drain you of strength and stamina. So be careful of his touch and never take your mask off. As far as Professor Ohm, we don't know what kind, but he may exhibit some supernatural ability, so be aware of that possibility also."

Carol said to the professor, "The look is not very fashionable. Perhaps I can help you design the next batch of masks. They are light and feel like cloth to the skin."

She pulled it over her head and grabbed her hair so it would come out from the bottom of the mask in the back to see the fit. They all tried the masks on and then took them off, except for Phillip, who was going to leave shortly. He was given the tracer and shown the best route to Jacob's camp. He put his communication device in his ear in a place designed in the mask and then took off to the mountain.

"This is your voice in the great Northwest, Matt Par, talking about the things of importance to you. We have an open line for your call on this talk radio network extravaganza show. Let's have a discussion, dialogue, conversation, an intelligent exchange of words about the beautiful area we call home.

"For years, we have lived with the presence of one of the most powerful destructive forces in nature in our backyard, namely Mount Rainier, an active volcano. Are we doing enough to keep the community safe from harm for the people in the Seattle and Tahoma area? Can we do more? What if we had a Mount Saint Helens–type explosion from the tallest volcano in Washington? Are you awake, people of Washington? Did you not see the clouds of steam from the top of this giant? It is beautiful, picturesque, but deadly under the right circumstances. We will talk to the experts and you about the inevitable eruption that will happen sometime in the future, but when?

"And in the second hour, we will talk about the attack on Pier 91. What is happening to solve the case about the explosion over the water and bombs planted on the pier itself? The police and Homeland Security are saying very little to the public about the incident. And what of the eyewitness reports about a man seen flying over the water just moments before the explosion? And what about the mysterious rumor of unusual activity in the baggage area and on the ramp to the ship? We will leave no stone unturned to satisfy your curiosity about the things that are important to you. This is Matt Par of the Northwest Radio Talk Network saying, don't touch that dial. We will be right back after these short messages."

Jane reached over to turn down the volume of the radio. She was entering the campus of the University of Washington and trying to find the Burke Museum of Natural History and Culture in Seattle. She wished she had time to hear what Matt Par and his listeners had to say about the incident at Pier 91, but her visit to the museum was more important right now. Mike Morris, her nerdy friend, had looked over hundreds of pictures and newsletters about the university, searching for a man named John with blond hair who graduated six years earlier. She was still looking for the mystery man called the Advocate who had saved her life in the attack by Jack Nash. With very little to go on, except for her brief look into the blue eyes of her savior, she needed a little luck to find John, which was the name Jack Nash called him. Mike had found an alumnus picture of a man donating some American Indian artifacts to the museum, who was named John.

Jane found a place to park. Then she went to the front desk and showed her newspaper ID and asked if she could talk to someone about the exhibit of Native American artifacts donated a couple of years before. The lady said that Peter Roth was the expert in that area of the museum, and she would see if he could talk to her right then. She called him in his office.

Peter said that he could spare a few minutes for Jane and came out to meet her.

"Hello, my name is Peter Roth. How can I help the *Gazette* today?"

He reached out to shake her hand, and he was pleasantly surprised he was looking at a beautiful woman. As Jane reached out to meet his handshake, she saw a middle-aged man about six feet one inch, dressed in a dark suit and blue tie. He had dark hair, except for the streaking of gray and white highlights. She got to the point. "I am interested in some Native American artifacts donated by a man named John two years ago to the museum. I don't have much more information than that. I could not make out his last name in the article I read."

"Well, we had several additions to our museum in that year. Why don't we walk over there and take a look?"

They walked toward the exhibition of ancient American history in the area and saw arrowheads, pottery, and many other additions to the museum from that year, but none of them had been donated by a man named John. Finally, Peter walked over to a spear and knife that he said was over 1,500 years old. They were remarkably well preserved right down to the bone blade and spearhead. The spear itself was very long and was in excellent shape for such old wood. Jane looked down at the engraved plaque that said, "Donated from the Tomar Estate by Nathan and John Tomar." She was excited when she saw the name John. She asked, "May I call you Peter?"

He nodded his head yes.

She continued, "Do you have a good picture of the donors somewhere?"

Peter thought for a moment and then said, "Why, yes, I think I do. Let me check the folder I have on the exhibit."

Peter and Jane walked back to his office, and he offered her a seat by his desk. She sat down, and he said, "This should only take a moment."

He looked in the file cabinet, found a folder, and set it on his desk. Jane was standing by then in anticipation of viewing the picture. Finally, Peter pulled out a eight-by-ten-inch picture and gave it to Jane. "Here it is."

In the picture, Jane saw a young man and an older man with Peter. Peter was presenting a certificate of recognition to the older man. The young man was tall and had blond hair. Jane's heart rate increased, and she smiled as she thought to herself, *That has to be him.* Then she said to Peter, "Do you have a copier? May I have a copy?"

Peter replied, "Yes, I have a copier right here, if you don't mind it on copy paper."

He opened the scanner to place the picture to be copied and then pushed the button. The scanner made a mechanical noise as it copied the picture. He handed the copy to her, and she looked at it again. Then Peter said, "Just what is this about, may I ask?"

Jane looked up to Peter, smiled, and said, "I believe the young man in the picture saved my life a short while ago, and I wanted to thank him but did not know how to find him. Thank you so much for your help. Do you know where the Tomar Estate is, Peter?"

Peter thought for a moment and then said, "I have never been there, but I think it is off Interstate 90 out of Seattle. I hope you find your savior and remember the museum kindly if you write about this."

Jane smiled, thanked Peter again, and then left, heading for her vehicle in the parking lot.

Chapter 11

Albert Hughes's Journal

The Genesis Project
Log Entry 19.5

The Genesis Factor has properties that are not just amazing but defy what we knew previously about life through science. It works not only on the gene and the microcell level but at the subatomic level also. It seems to unlock abilities in humans that I feel have remained dormant for thousands of years. These latent levels of control are added in their strength by the mind of the individual and his or her belief of the power it displays. The end result is not only unlimited power but matter and energy manipulation itself.

Aiko Sakura has already learned how to manipulate energy. She has created a force from the kinetic energy of an attacker to repel him and, I believe, can tap into electric, magnetic, and chemical energy also. The heat of her brother Hiroki is his way of manipulating the energy that is around him at all times. The way he creates heat is the way he makes the air around him cool so the heat does not burn him. Time and practice have taught him how to control his power. The potential here for improving energy manipulation is limited only by the individual's mind.

All the others have this same potential and ability to get better in their power levels. Even Samuel Touré has the ability in him to manifest other powers besides superstrength and stamina. I have tried to explain this to them one-on-one, but the belief in this possibility is up to them to work out for themselves. John has shown the greatest control of energy and matter manipulation of all those tested. His mind has great discipline and faith in his abilities. I believe he has the ability to grow even beyond his present state of control.

Now, Nathan is a mystery to me. He will not submit to the normal testing that the others have been put through, but I can guess he may be a master in energy and matter manipulation. The large men in the trailer had him subdued and were going to rip his arms off, but he slipped through their grasp and used his own body as a weapon to hit them over the head. My guess is he manipulated the atoms in his arms to become intangible to set himself free, and then he made his hands as hard as granite and struck them to give himself time to get away and check on the others. As previously reported, he has lived hundreds of years and knows more about how to use the powers that the substance provides than anyone.

In conclusion, I consider it a privilege to be a part of the study. I know I have only scratched the surface of possibilities. There is a finite amount of substance, so I need to go to the cave of origin to study more about how it came to earth. I believe it is not of this world, but is not a totally alien substance either. My conjecture is that it is from a higher existence or reality, and it did not originate from here but possibly another dimension. While I have no concrete proof of this speculation, it is the only explanation of the supernatural manifestations in humans. I have enjoyed getting to know all those involved in the Genesis Project and hope that the upcoming crisis on Mount Rainier will not injure or kill any of them.

I pray to God that their abilities and Nathan's wisdom are enough to overcome the conflict at the mountain and bring to an end the insane attempt of Jacob Starr and Professor Ohm to start a volcanic explosion in Mount Rainier. The clock is ticking, and we have less than twenty-four hours before their attempt to change the life for hundreds of thousands of people in Washington State. See log entry 18.1 where I discuss the unusual powers that Jacob and those around him have exhibited in this conflict.

The truck came to a stop about three miles from the trailer location in a clearing. There was a ten-by-fifteen-foot tent erected with a pitched roof. Centurion pulled the tent door to the side and tied the straps to hold both sides open. He then raised the ramp to the bed of the truck. The men offered to help him into the back of the truck, but he told them to stay put. He walked into the back and then picked up and carried a large box about eight feet long and three feet wide over his shoulder. Under the wood frame, it looked like it was covered in lead. If it was an old Russian warhead, it had to weigh about two thousand pounds, and Centurion was carrying it fairly easily. He took it to the ramp and lowered it to the ground; then he set it on a steel frame on wheels with rubber tires and pulled the payload into the tent.

Phillip had followed the truck with little difficulty and attached the homing device to a tree on the north side of the clearing. Then he hit the button on the device, telling the others that the truck had finally reached its destination. After that, he got a text message sent from his satellite phone on his belt that read: "Keep a low profile and watch the activities of the site. We will be there a half-mile west of you in one hour. Contact you then."

Phillip looked around and found a comfortable place to hide while he watched the twenty men who came in the trucks and the big guy in the tent. He figured their boss and the professor would be along shortly.

Jane could not wait for Mike to give her an exact location of the Tomar Estate, and now she was lost in the small community of Cle Elum off Interstate 90. She was in a coffee shop in the town. The waitress seated her, and she then asked if she could help her. Jane said, "Yes, I will have a cup of coffee, please."

The waitress replied, "Coming right up."

Jane's phone rang. She fumbled in her purse and then finally pulled it out and answered the call. It was Mike Morris. He told her, "I can't find an address for the Tomar Estate, but the Cle Elum post office is where they pick up their mail. Perhaps you can get more information from the locals there. Ask someone in the community."

"Well, I'll start with the coffee shop and work from there. Bye, Mike."

The waitress brought the coffee to the table at that moment, and Jane asked, "What's your name?"

The waitress set the coffee down, smiled, and said, "My name is Connie. You need anything else?"

Jane smiled back and said, "My name is Jane. Glad to meet you. Have you ever heard of the Tomar Estate in this area?"

Connie thought for a moment and then said, "I am new to this town. Don't know where it might be, but Charley might know. He's been driving a truck for some time in this area and is having breakfast at the counter."

Connie pointed toward a man with a Seahawks ball cap on his head and a long-sleeve shirt, wearing blue jeans. Then she yelled at the man, "Hey, Charley, this woman has a question for you. Mind if she joins you? Her name is Jane."

Charley looked in that direction and said, "Sure. I'd be a fool to turn down the company of a pretty woman. Come on over."

Connie picked up the cup of coffee and walked toward Charley. Jane picked her purse up and headed to the counter also. She felt uneasy and was wondering what she had gotten herself into.

Jane sat down, put her purse at her feet, and then looked at Charley. "Thanks for talking to me. Connie says you know the area very well. Can you direct me to the Tomar Estate?"

Charley smiled and put down his cup of coffee. "People around these parts are pretty private, and many don't like visitors. What is your business with them?"

Jane looked down and then right into his eyes and said, "Charley, I was attacked and John Tomar saved my life, but left before I could say thank you properly. I have been looking for him for some time. It is very personal for me."

Charley looked at her intently for a moment, took his hat off, and set it on the counter. Then he replied, "My guess is you're telling the truth, but I can't help you. I told the old man Tomar that I would not give his location to a stranger, and that is who you are. Sorry, ma'am."

Jane's heart sank. She was devastated. A wave of anxiety came over her, and she started to tear up, but she was not going to let it stop her. She stopped the emotional accelerator and said, "Charley, you don't understand. I was stabbed by the Seattle Slasher, but he saved me and stopped the murder spree. The killer is now awaiting trial because of him."

Charley pointed his finger at her and said, "You're that reporter for the *Seattle Gazette*. Read your story. Don't remember anything about you being saved in the story, much less about you being stabbed. The cops said he was out cold when they got there in another paper's article."

Jane shook her head and was wondering how far she had to go to convince him to tell her. She said finally, "Just forget it. Thanks for your time, Charley."

She started to reach down to get her purse.

He looked at her and said, "Just a minute, missy. Follow me to my truck. I have something I want to show you." He put enough money on the counter to pay for his meal and her coffee with a generous tip and then said, "Here, Connie. Thanks for breakfast."

"Anytime, Charley."

Charley put his hat on and started out the door. He looked back at Jane, who was still sitting there, and said, "You coming?"

When Jane got to his truck, Charley opened the cab of his tractor and pulled out a box from behind his seat. He was pretty high up and then stepped to the ground with a picture that he gave to Jane. She looked at a picture of another truck with a load of large lumber that had fallen from the trailer, and it was in a pile on the ground with some of the logs still hanging in the trailer. He then said to Jane, "I was securing my load of lumber when another driver jackknifed his trailer going too fast and dumped his load on me near the Tomar Estate. I was buried under the weight of trees. My body was crushed. I felt my heart stopping when the old man Tomar and John came out of nowhere. John pulled the largest log off me as if it was nothing. Tomar grabbed my hand and pulled me right through the other log that still was on my legs. I was semiconscious most of the time until I recovered. Then I looked up at Tomar and John with very little pain in spite of having several tons of lumber on me. It was a miracle, but Tomar and John acted as if I had just gotten knocked out and the wind taken from my lungs. However, I know the truth. I was dying, and they saved my life. Bet your story is the same with the attack of this Nash guy. Am I right?"

Jane felt as if a weight had been lifted from her. Someone had experienced the same miracle of life. Charley had also been saved from sure death. She was in tears, relieved to find someone who would believe her story. She said to Charley, "Yes, I was bleeding with the knife of the Slasher in my gut when John pulled him off me, put his hand on my wound, and healed me. The trauma of that moment haunts me to this day. Thank you for telling me your story."

Charley then grabbed her hand and said to her, "You know you can never tell my story or yours to the public, and you can't print it in the paper. People are not ready to believe in miracles—not most anyway."

The reality of what he had said went against Jane's reporter's ethics, but she knew he was right and conceded, "Yes, I see that now they must be left alone to do their good works without the public knowing. It is how they work best. The government or corporations or special interest would exploit them and use them for their purposes. I could never get enough proof for everyone to accept them without controlling them. If that means that I can't see John's blue eyes again or thank him for what he did, so be it."

Charley seemed touched by what she had said and asked her, "You have feelings for the young man, don't you?"

Jane thought for a moment and then said, "I guess I do. Now that you say that, yes, I guess I do."

Charley reached behind the seat again and pulled out an old map. He gave it to her and then said, "The second gate on the way up the mountain is hard to open, but there is a mechanical solar-powered motor that will open it for you. The switch is behind the right post. Have a nice life, Jane."

He then climbed into the cab of his truck and started the diesel engine. Jane stepped away from the truck, and he took off honking his horn in two short bursts. She walked back to her car in the parking lot and folded out the map that Charley had given her on her hood. She saw a mark on the map that said "Tomar Estate." It was just north of her location in the backwoods. She smiled and thought, *Finally.*

Tomar's plan was simple: launch a full assault on the remote location, subduing the twenty men without killing them, and take control of the nuclear device—the key part of Professor Ohm's plan.

His hope was to get it done before Jacob and the professor could arrive. Phillip had taken a picture of the clearing with the nuclear device and sent it on his phone to the others. Tomar and John had studied the area and informed the others of their responsibilities at the site.

Tomar, John, Carol, Aiko, Samuel, and Hiroki arrived by helicopter in a small clearing near Phillip's location. Phillip met them a half-mile west of the group of men. All the group had camouflage jumpsuits on and were wearing the masks that Albert Hughes had made for them. Tomar raised his hand and said, "Each of you knows your assignment. If you do not, please speak up now. Activate your communication devices in your masks. I want you to use your code names when addressing one another."

Samuel asked, "What is your code name and John's one more time?"

Carol hit Samuel on the shoulder and said, "That's easy, Samson. Tomar is called Griz, and John is called Advocate. Right, John?"

John smiled and said, "That's right, Carol—I mean, Jag—and Aiko is Siphon; Hiroki is Sol; Samuel is Samson, and of course, Phillip is Aero."

Tomar said, "All right, let's get serious here. I want you to use all your ability to stay alive. The faster you make your adversary lose consciousness, the quicker we get control of the camp and end the threat to the people in the area. Jag, remember the air pistol tranquilizer darts must hit in the skin to work, and, Aero, the Taser disks work best when placed on the spine of your opponent. Keep your masks on at all times. They make you invisible to Jacob, and we would like to avoid his involvement if we can help it."

John added, "Remember, these are trained military, and they do not use tranq darts or Tasers; they shoot bullets and use knives. They would kill you if you let them. Help one another out, and cover one another's back."

The group moved into position on the north side of the camp, and then they split up. John, Samuel, and Hiroki came in from the

east. Tomar, Carol, and Aiko came in from the west. Since Phillip
was the fastest, he came in from the north.

No one had spotted anyone in the group yet. Centurion was
in the tent getting the nuke ready for the professor. He was taking
the outer wood frame off and removing the lead shielding it was
packaged in. He was almost done when Tomar said, "Move now!"
into the communication device. Phillip, in superspeed mode, hit
six men on the north side of the tent with the Tasers. He properly
placed the Tasers on their backs, and the men were immobilized.
Then Tomar hit two men on the head and laid them out cold. Carol
shot three men who were drawing their guns in the neck with the
tranquilizer darts, and they passed out. Aiko used the energy around
her to throw two men against the truck. They hit their heads and
were out. Phillip would tie the hands and feet of the downed men
with plastic zip ties, so they could not enter the fight later.

John, Samuel, and Hiroki concentrated on the four men on the
east side of the camp. Samuel picked two men up and knocked their
heads together. Hiroki heated the guns the other two had pulled,
and they dropped the weapons. John gave them his version of the
Vulcan mind pinch and told them to go to sleep, which they did.
The remaining three men jumped into the tent with Centurion and
pulled their guns. They started firing in any direction. Carol was
hit in the arm, and Aiko was hit in the stomach. As Aiko fell, her
brother Hiroki shot flames out and burned the tent with the men
and Centurion still in there. The shooting stopped, but Centurion
grabbed the frame and threw the tent in the air. Hiroki finished
burning the tent, and it floated in ashes to the ground in the camp
area.

The men who were standing around the nuke pulled their
guns again and began shooting, but suddenly, there was a loud
shout, "Stop!" and the men stopped. Then they fell to the ground
asleep. Phillip confiscated their guns and tied their hands and feet.
Everyone looked at John, who had pulled his mask off so he could

use his mental powers to control the men. They all, except for Tomar, looked amazed by the exhibition of John's power.

John immediately ran over to Aiko with her brother right behind him to see how she was. She was bleeding badly and almost unconscious.

Hiroki was very upset and said, "Help her, please."

John grabbed Hiroki's hand and said, "It's going to be all right."

Then, with everyone watching, he used his power to reach inside her body and surgically pull the slug out of her. He threw it to the ground. After that, he placed his hand on the bloody area of her stomach. After a few moments, she opened her eyes. She looked up at John and said, "Thank you, John. I knew you would come."

John did the same for Carol, who was in great pain. The bullet had gone clean through her arm and shattered her bone. The warmth of his touch healed her arm.

Tomar was working on the nuke to neutralize the threat of an explosion. He was sending pictures of the warhead to Albert Hughes. Albert responded, "From the pictures and serial number, it looks like the Russian model SS-18 Satan, between two to five megatons, very lethal. We must separate the primary device from the secondary bomb, which will render the secondary larger explosion impossible and stop the chance of Jacob succeeding in his plan. I will instruct you on how to do that."

Phillip had fetched the toolbox, and Tomar finished taking the outer casing off the bomb. It was on rails that led to a tunnel just large enough for the device to slide to the heart of the volcano. It was attached to a winch and cable. The tunnel was smooth, like it had been created by a high-powered laser, and was steep enough to let gravity send the bomb to its destination.

Albert communicated to Tomar, "The tunnel must lead to that strategic spot in the volcano to release the full energy of the nuke and create a volcanic explosion many times greater than the bomb, blowing the top right off the mountain. The power needed to create the tunnel would be amazing. I wonder how the professor did it."

As Tomar was starting to remove the primary firing device from the nuke, John walked up and said to him, "Jacob is on his way. Evidently, the big guy communicated with him before we could subdue him. I sense three other people with him. Professor Ohm, the other big guy they call Legion, and Trevor the head of the private military force. Also, he just radioed the eighty men at the other location and told them to head this way. The men will be here in about thirty-five minutes, but Jacob and the others will be here in ten minutes is my guess. I am already feeling Jacob's influence mentally."

"Can you block him?"

"I think so, for a while; the closer he gets, the more I can feel him. What are we going to do?"

Tomar looked right at John and said, "Work as fast as I can to disarm the bomb and pray we can get it done in time."

Chapter 12

"I am Captain McNair of the Second Stryker Brigades of the Second Infantry Division from Lewis-McChord. What are you armed men doing on the mountain? Who authorized you to take up arms and occupy this camp?"

Trevor's second in command, Howard Wagner, was responding to his order to mobilize the men to the other location. The men were gathering their gear and weapons and getting ready to move to the other site when six army vehicles blocked the road. There were three infantry carrier vehicles with a fifty-caliber gun and a grenade launcher, each with an infantry squad and their fighting equipment, one mobile gun system vehicle with a 105-millimeter cannon, one commander vehicle with a fifty-caliber gun and a grenade launcher, and the Growler scout vehicle that Captain McNair stepped out of to talk.

Wagner responded to the captain, "Captain McNair, we are part of the private military contractor GK Starr out of Washington, DC, and are authorized by the Department of Defense to help Starr Corp with security for the project on Mount Rainier. Here is my ID, Captain."

Wagner handed him his ID. The captain said to Wagner, "This military security exercise was not registered with the United States military in the region. And this ground has been scorched with an explosion. Can you tell me what that is about?"

The men were getting anxious, and the captain could hear them murmuring. Wagner said, "Captain, it is important for us to move out right now. We have orders to mobilize to a different location. Our operation is of the utmost importance. If you let us leave, we can explain to the US military later."

The captain tossed the ID card back at Wagner and then pointed his finger at him and said, "Be careful what you do or say at this point, Howard Wagner. I have a hundred men in the trees waiting for my order for them to move on this location, and I can get air support here at my command in less than twenty minutes. I am going to give you new orders authorized by the head of military forces in Washington State, General Wade Eiling. I want your men to gather all the weapons and put them in a pile right in front of my vehicle. I want every gun, knife, nail cutter—*every* weapon and communication device in the group of men. Then I want them to sit on the ground in groups of ten until I sort out this mess. Is that clear, Wagner?"

Wagner realized it was futile to try to convince the captain to let them go, and he said, "Yes, sir, Captain."

Then he walked back, yelling to the group leaders to comply with the captain's orders. Wagner whispered into his mouthpiece on his chest as he walked away, "We are not going to make it, Trevor."

Trevor acknowledged to Wagner that he had heard the whole conversation. Then he looked at Jacob, who was in the SUV with Professor Ohm and Legion, Jacob's muscle man. "They are not coming; the US Army has detained them. Someone must have called them."

Although the battery was low in the drone on the trailer, the camera was able to film the arrival of the US Army—but with no sound. Nacu relayed that information to Tomar in his communication device. "Tomar, the army has stopped the rest of the men in the group from moving to your location, but Jacob, Professor Ohm, their second in command, and the other big guy are not here. They are probably near or at your location by now."

John had rearranged twenty-one men in bonds and made sure they would not be awake too soon. He put double bonds on Centurion. Tomar had finally loosened the primary firing mechanism from the housing of the bomb, and he was about to remove it from the nuclear material. He responded to the call by Nacu and then said to John, "Can you still sense Jacob nearby? Is he close?"

"Yes, they are watching us right now, waiting for the right moment to attack, take over the camp, and reactivate the bomb. I am able to monitor the others' minds. They are talking right now about what to do, but Jacob is reaching out to me, trying to read my mind, and I am blocking him. He is very strong. I am sure I can block him for now. I can't enter his mind; that would give him access to mine. They are talking about a diversion, so they can rush the bomb. Professor, are you getting this? Do you have a suggestion as to what to do?"

Everyone but John still had the mental inhibiting masks on. Professor Hughes said, "Once you separate the primary firing mechanism from the nuclear material, cut the cable and let it go down the shaft to the lava flow at 1,800 to 2,200 degrees; it will assimilate into the volcano and be harmless at that point."

Tomar added, "That will get rid of the evidence that proves that Jacob is trying to kill thousands of people."

The professor argued, "Yes, but better that happen than risk the chance of them setting it off under the right circumstances for an eruption. Also, destroy the control panel that is next to the bomb, so there is no chance of that happening."

Tomar reluctantly agreed, "Okay, Albert, we will do it your way, but what about the primary firing mechanism? It can be ignited also with a considerable explosion."

The professor replied, "Once you separate the primary firing mechanism, we will remove the compression and electronic detonating device from the warhead, and it will not fire, but you need to separate it from the main nuclear material first."

Suddenly, John yelled to the group, "Take cover! They're coming!"

Just then, the SUV came out of the trees right at them. Legion was driving, and Trevor was shooting a rapid-fire gun in their direction out his window. Everyone except Tomar and John hit the ground. John blocked every shot with his telekinesis and then, with an invisible hand, turned the vehicle on its side. With this going on, Jacob and Professor Ohm came in from the other direction and met Carol and Aiko, who were on the ground first. Jacob touched them in the back. They both felt weak and then fell unconscious on the ground. Phillip saw what had happened, got up, and ran at the pair at superspeed, but electricity shot out from Professor Ohm's hands, acting like a giant Taser and rendering him incapacitated. Jacob touched him also to tell him to go to sleep. It was now four against four. At the SUV, Legion had climbed out of the side of the vehicle, jumped down, and grabbed a giant boulder he'd found. He threw it at John. John, with his power, easily blocked the boulder, sending it to the ground, and knocked him off his feet.

Trevor climbed out of the vehicle and put another clip in his gun. He started shooting again. Hiroki had had enough of that. He got up and heated the air around him. He flew toward Trevor and melted the gun in his hands. Trevor screamed out in pain and threw the gun down. He grabbed his knife on his belt and threw it at Hiroki, striking him in his left arm. Hiroki was in pain. He flew toward Trevor and hit him in the chest with his good arm and then twisted his body and kicked him in the groin. He had promised Tomar he would not kill, so instead of burning the life from him, he hit him with a hammer punch across the jaw and knocked him out. Then he pulled the knife from his shoulder and cauterized the wound to stop the bleeding.

At the same time all this was going on, Samuel was getting up. He ran toward Legion to stop his advance toward the bomb. Legion was charging like a bull and hit him with his forearm. The force was like a speeding freight train; it knocked him on his rear. It looked like Samuel had met his match in strength.

He jumped up and hit Legion as hard as he could in the face, but he just shook his head, laughed, and taunted him, "Is that the best you can do? I have the strength of a thousand men. You don't have a chance."

Then he remembered John's training. When you meet someone of great strength, you find their weakness. He had worked for hours with John locating those vulnerable points. He remembered John's words: *"Everyone has vulnerable points; you just have to find them."*

Then he noticed that Legion had a very big forehead, which was one of the pressure points. He hit him there with the bottom of his palm. The blow knocked his head back, exposing what little neck he had. Samuel hit the side of his neck with a karate chop that snapped his head to the left. This move exposed his rib cage. Samuel stepped toward Legion and hit him in his exposed ribs with his fist as hard as he could. He could feel the ribs breaking on that side, which made Legion grimace in pain, and he exposed the left side of his jaw. Samuel, with a powerful adrenaline rush and determination to win, increased in size and strength. This time, when he hit him in the jaw, he broke it and knocked him out cold. Legion fell to the ground.

Back at the bomb, Tomar and John had their hands full. Professor Ohm was sending bolts of lightning from his hands, which John was having a hard time blocking with his power. Every time he tried to control the professor mentally to stop him, Jacob intercepted him to protect his partner. Tomar jumped at Jacob and engaged him in hand-to-hand combat. Tomar was a master at every fighting skill known to man, but he was really challenged by Jacob with every move. And every time Jacob touched him, he could feel strength leave him. He did not know how long he could keep this up, but the attention he could get from Jacob helped John with his fight against Professor Ohm. John began to gain the upper hand with the professor by forcing him back to the truck. John could feel his thoughts now with Jacob busy. Then the professor pulled the canvas cover off a piece of equipment that looked like a cannon. The group had seen this before, but they were not concerned because it had no power source. He put his hands on the two handles, aimed it at John, and then released a powerful laser that almost hit him, but instead, he disintegrated the lower half of a hundred-year-old pine tree nearby, and it fell to the ground. The professor aimed it at Tomar, who had become lighter than air, to evade Jacob's attack and regain his strength. He was about ten feet in the air when the professor fired the laser. It was a direct hit on Tomar, who just disappeared and was no more.

John yelled, "No!"

John was in shock and could not accept what had just happened. He reacted in anger and lifted the professor and the laser in the air with his power. He noticed that all electrical activity had stopped, and the laser was powerless when he was in the air. John realized that Professor Ohm got his powers from contact with the earth. John then threw the professor against the truck and knocked him out. After this, he looked at Jacob, who was furious at what had just happened to the professor. Jacob sensed the opening in John's mind. The emotional trauma of seeing Tomar's death had opened his mind to Jacob's power, and he attacked him hard mentally. John felt his nervous system shutting down. He could not move. It was like before, and then he felt his heart rate increase. Jacob was trying to induce a heart attack in John. The pain was excruciating. He felt like he was truly going to die. Then he thought of Tomar and remembered the relaxation exercise he had taught him when he was out of control. He closed his eyes and visited that area of tranquility and peace he had created in his mind years ago and regained his composure. His heart rate returned to normal, and he could move his body once again. He then pushed Jacob from his mind.

Jacob looked surprised and said in a loud voice, "You cannot resist me; I have never met my equal in the mind."

John said back to him, "Never say never."

They both stood there looking at each other. John then attempted to enter Jacob's mind. Jacob allowed him to enter him psychically. They both shut their eyes and prepared to meet in the Mindscape of Jacob's psychic world. It was dark at first, and John saw a silhouette of a man in front of a reddish light. A voice came from the figure, "You should never have come to this place. I am the supreme ruler here, and you are going to die."

"I guess you shouldn't have left your door open. What is this thing you have with the word *never*? You ended the life of the greatest, kindest man I have ever known, and for that, you are going down."

The voice from the shadow continued, "That's right. You could not protect him. The group of people you brought with you will fail, and I will defeat you and then the others and blow you all up with this mountain, leaving no evidence you ever existed much less the good you tried to do. Now you are going to be humiliated."

John bowed his head and then prayed right in front of Jacob's shadow, "Anonius was the name my father called you, and *Ye-shua* is what Eli calls you. I call you Lord; you have not given us the spirit of fear but of power and of love and of a sound mind. Help me to honor that right now, Lord. Help me in this. What I do, I do for you and the memory of Tomar."

Jacob heard the prayer and was furious. He sent hundreds of knives at John. John sent them back at the shadow of Jacob, and they passed right through him like he was a ghost. Jacob said to John from his shadow, "It is time to end this."

The shadow began to grow and took on the form of a giant dragon. The light behind the creature became brighter as the figure became three-dimensional, showing the claws and wings and the monstrous size of his legs and arms. The dragon flapped his wings and flew at him, shooting fire from his mouth. John began to glow in the darkness of Jacob's mind, and armor materialized in the Mindscape with a large shield and blocked the fire of the dragon. The flames shot around him. He pulled out a sword of fire and dived at the dragon, piercing his heart. Jacob screamed very loud, and John left his mind. While Jacob was in pain, John flew at him in the physical world and hit him in the jaw, causing a concussion, and Jacob lost consciousness.

While this was happening, Hiroki and Samuel were working on the bomb and in communication with Professor Hughes. Hughes had convinced them that it was more important to neutralize the bomb and save thousands of lives than to join the fight against Jacob and Professor Ohm. Samuel pulled the primary firing mechanism from the nuclear material, and then he set it on a table. Under Hughes's instruction, Hiroki burned the cable, and the main part of the bomb flew down the shaft. Samuel, with the help of Professor Hughes, turned on the monitor of the instrument panel, and they watched as it went over two thousand feet into the lava. At this time, Professor Ohm blasted Tomar with the laser, and he disappeared.

Grief hit them, and they both started to leave the bomb.

Samuel said, "We are done here. Tomar is gone. The professor blasted him with a laser, and John is alone."

Professor Hughes yelled into the communication device, "No! John can take care of himself. You need to finish what you are doing. Send the primary firing device down the shaft also."

Hiroki and Samuel looked at each other. They agreed that John could prevail and continued. Samuel removed the compression and the electronic detonating devices from what was left of the warhead, put the primary firing device on a small dolly they had found, and sent it down the shaft.

When it was several hundred feet into the shaft, Professor Hughes said, "Burn the entrance to the shaft, and destroy the equipment at the site so it cannot be used again."

Samuel picked up a large boulder and threw it down the shaft. Hiroki melted the control panel and area around the opening until it was closed, and then Samuel threw the laser cannon at the now covered hole. Hiroki melted that into a puddle of metal.

John joined them after taking care of Jacob and said, "Let's wake up the others and go home."

He woke up Phillip, Carol, and Aiko, and they secured Jacob's legs and hands and then put one of the mental inhibiting masks over his head to keep him from using his power if he woke up. They made sure the others were also not going to interfere with them leaving.

Aiko looked intently at John and said, "Where is Tomar?"

John looked at the ground. Tears began to form in his eyes. He looked up into her eyes and said, "He is gone. Professor Ohm shot him with a laser, and he is no more."

Aiko cried out, "No! Not him! He did not want to hurt anybody, just save lives. Why him?"

Tears flowed from Aiko's and Carol's eyes.

Phillip said, "An eye for an eye. We should—"

John interrupted Phillip and said in a loud voice, "No, Tomar wanted to save lives. Life was precious to him. We will not kill this day. Finish what you are doing, and then let's leave. Our job is done here."

Phillip continued, "You know these bonds won't hold them for very long. If the army doesn't come quickly they will be gone."

John answered, "I know, but I will not kill them, and we can't take them with us. They were defeated at a great cost. Do the best you can in securing them."

Professor Albert Hughes contacted Phillip on another channel and asked him to do something for him over the communicator after he was awakened by John and before they left. Then Hughes looked at Nacu and said, "I can't believe he's gone. To live so long and then die like that, what a shame!"

Nacu was deep in grief and distressed by what had happened. He said, "I have lost my brother and friend. I wish it would have been me who died instead of him. I was an outcast, shunned by my tribe, when he took me in and saved me."

The sky was getting dark, and clouds were rolling in by then. Another storm was coming. It would be raining soon. John called his friend at Lewis-McChord and let them know where to find the small camp with Jacob and the others. John had taken the compression and electronic detonating device from the Russian warhead with him, but he did not know whom he could show in the government to convince them that Jacob was going to kill thousands of people. He did not know whom he could trust, and he already missed his father, Tomar, and his solid advice. He said to the others, "Pick up our equipment, and let's go home."

A car pulled up to the gate of the Tomar Estate. A young lady got out of the car and walked up to the gate. She looked for some way to communicate to the occupants inside. She found a button and speaker on the right side of the gate and pushed it. She looked up and saw a security camera zoom in on her. Then she heard a voice over the speaker ask, "May I help you?"

The lady answered, "Hello, my name is Jane Watkins; I need to speak to John. It is important. Can you help me?"

The voice hesitated in answering for a few seconds and then said, "I'm sorry, Ms. Watkins; he is not home right now."

She looked disappointed and said, "Please, is there a way I can leave him a message?"

The voice from the speaker said, "Why, yes, look into the camera above and leave your message anytime you want. I will record it for him to see."

Jane looked at the camera and said, "Thank you." Then she left a detailed message, which Nacu recorded for John to watch later. After that, she walked back to her car as it started to rain. She pulled away and left the gate of the Tomar Estate.

Chapter 13

"Captain McNair, there is no one here. There is evidence of a struggle and battle, but no men are in this place at this time. There are tire tracks and a pile of metal that is still warm from an extreme amount of heat. There are shell casings and other signs that something went on here of a military nature."

Lieutenant Scott radioed the captain from the two infantry carrier vehicles sent by Captain McNair to investigate the report of gunfire at a location near them.

He responded, "Get as much evidence as you can, and take pictures of the area for the general. Then report back here."

The lieutenant responded, "Yes, sir, Captain."

None of Jacob's men were to be found in the area, and he and Professor George Ohm were on their way off the mountain to plan another day. They had escaped their bonds at the smaller site and left. Jacob was already on the phone to his contact at the Department of Defense to minimize his failure at the mountain. His Project Tahoma had failed, but he was not going to be indicted for simply protecting the scientific exploration of the mountain. With the evidence of the nuclear device gone, he could escape with his dignity still intact. He was just protecting the mountain from a hostile force. Captain McNair had just now received orders to release the military force at the trailer. A truck ordered by Jacob was on its way to get the trailer at the original site and take it to his Portland office.

"Are you okay, Jacob?" Professor Ohm asked him in the beat-up SUV on its way to the airport.

Jacob was truly shaken mentally and emotionally by his encounter at the mountain with the blond man. As hard as it was to admit he had met his match in every way, the words of Madam Scarlet La Brasa came back to him: "There is a secret group of people who will interfere with your plans and a man who will challenge you in your conquest of power; he is your match in will and strength."

After a few seconds of thought, Jacob said to Professor Ohm, "I am fine, Professor. How is your head?"

The professor answered, "Once I woke up and put my feet on the ground, I felt better. Who are those remarkable people we ran into at the mountain?

Jacob looked out the window and said, "I don't know, but even though we failed in our objective at the mountain, we hurt the group to the core. We took the life of their leader, Tomar. Once I fix the little problem with the army and the Department of Defense, we will make it our priority to find out who they are. One by one, they will pay. Their unwillingness to kill will be their undoing."

Aiko cried out, "The pain does not go away! How do we go on without him?"

Aiko and Carol were there talking to Professor Hughes.

He responded to their grief, "The pain is real, and I share it with you. Grieving for a loved one takes awhile to recover from, but they are always a part of your life. Let your emotions do what is natural at times like this. I miss him also."

The ladies were in tears, and they reached out to embrace each other. The responsibility of counseling them fell on Professor Hughes.

John was with Hiroki and Samuel in the hangar bay. He had just checked the wound that Trevor had inflicted on Hiroki. It was almost healed, but the hearts of all were broken by the loss of Tomar. That would not be easily healed.

Samuel said, "What are we going to do now without Tomar?"

John responded, "We will grieve for Tomar for a while and then decide what the future of this gathering of people will be. Together, we went to the mountain, and together, we will decide our future with the help of God."

John embraced Samuel and then Hiroki.

Nacu was checking the helicopter, and Phillip was with him. Phillip interrupted Nacu's work and said, "Hey, mate, are you okay over here by yourself?"

"Better I do what has to be done, less time to think about what happened on that mountain. I will be all right, but a part of me died up there with Tomar. I feel like less of a man."

Phillip put his hand on Nacu's shoulder and said, "He was a good man. No one else could talk me into traveling over seven thousand miles and joining him in this gathering of young people. I have seen good men die before, but never has it got to me like Tomar. However, this is not about me. It was the ideals of one man and his example in life that drew me here. I am not saying that these ideals died with him, but I need to get away for a while."

Phillip handed Nacu a paper bag and said, "This is for the professor. Tell him each sample is marked with the name and description of the person I took it from. I will be gone for about a week. That should be long enough to decide what I am going to do."

Nacu asked Phillip, "You and John are good friends. What should I tell him?"

Phillip smiled and then said, "Tell John I am going on a walkabout. He will understand."

"Well, I found him, the one I've been looking for."

It was evening, and Jane was talking to Mike Morris. Jane had asked Mike to meet her at the Twilight Bar and Restaurant to discuss what she had found. She had to reflect on the day's activities. Mike was having a beer, and Jane was having a glass of red wine.

Mike put his bottle of beer down and asked, "You saw him? Is he the man who saved you from Jack Nash?"

"I am sure he is. I did not see him in person, but I found his house—I mean his *mansion*. The guy who answered the intercom let me leave a message for him because he was not there at the time."

Mike looked puzzled and said, "Then how do you know it is him, and how will you verify it is the John we are looking for?"

"It is a feeling more than anything. I know it is him, but I left it up to him to meet with me. I made an offer I hope he does not refuse, but I gave him a way out, told him if he did not want to meet me, he could call and cancel and I would understand."

Mike was amazed. "Jane Watkins, why are you giving him a way out? I thought you wanted to reveal him as your savior and a superhero."

"Well, things change. I realized he did much good without people knowing who he is, and if I take that away from him, he may stop helping people. That would be a shame. The world is not ready to accept a real-life superhero. So let him have the shadows to do what he does. Let him be a mystery to everyone and surprise the bad guys. If he wanted to be known, he would have revealed himself a long time ago."

Mike took a drink of his beer, looked at Jane, and then said, "Do you think he will see you? If he does not, will you pursue this any further?"

Jane twirled the wine in her glass and then said, "I hope he sees me, but if he does not, I will leave him alone and admire his work from afar, I guess."

Mike laughed and asked, "Who are you, and what did you do to the real Jane Watkins?"

Jane smiled and replied, "No, it's really me. I am thinking straighter than I have in years. My journey to find him revealed to me that there are more important things in this world than *the story*. People are what matter. Their lives count for something. Thank you, Mike, for being there for me and being a good friend. You helped me through a tough time in my life."

Mike smiled and raised his bottle to give a toast. Jane raised her glass of wine, and they tapped the glass and bottle. Mike said as they touched drinks, "To friendship."

"Professor, you mean you had Phillip gather some evidence at the site of the battle between Jacob's team and us so you could evaluate what we will be up against if we meet them in the future?"

John and Albert Hughes were in the laboratory.

Professor Hughes answered, "Yes, I should have more information about them in a couple of days, about the extent of their powers and the source, if I can."

John then said, "Sorry, Albert, I am not myself with the loss of my father. He was the rock in my life, even though he was not my biological father."

"Nathan told me that, but I never brought the subject up. I knew you would talk about it when you were ready. How did he meet your mother, and when did he adopt you?"

John answered, "He married my mother just after I was born and gave me his name through adoption. Never had the time to find out who my real father was, and I did not know my mother. Tomar said she died in Chicago suddenly, and there was no chance to save her."

"You started your life in tragedy, losing your mother, but you were raised with love by your proper father, Nathanial Tomar. Even though he was not your biological father, no one could have done a better job as a father than Nathan. I have never met a more honorable man than he."

Just then, Nacu walked into the room. He said, "I am sorry; I did not mean to interrupt your conversation."

John said, "I think we're done. What's up?"

Nacu answered, "I have something to show you, John. Tomar wanted me to give you this if something ever happened to him." Nacu had a tied leather-bound scroll that looked very old. He handed it to John and said, "There are many more in his room in a chest by his bed. This one is the latest. They are yours to read when you are ready. He told me they were his personal diary of the events of his life. He wanted you alone to have them. His life was rich and full. I am glad I have been part of it."

John replied, "Thank you, Nacu. You have been a friend and mentor of mine. Your devotion to Tomar, his ideas, and his life have been an example to me. When I felt like rebelling against what he said, there you were, loyal to the end. You are part of my family forever."

Nacu smiled and said, "That's not all, John. I have a video message for you to see. Someone came all the way to the mansion to leave it."

Looking perplexed, John said, "Really? We don't get a lot of visitors out here. Where can I view it?"

"If you are finished with the professor, follow me to the control room, and I will show it to you."

Professor Hughes smiled and said, "I'm done with you, John; go see your message."

John and Nacu left and headed for the security control room. In the room, there were several monitors showing security cameras all over the property. Nacu walked him over to one of the bigger monitor screens that was blank and said, "To view the message, just hit the play button on the keyboard when you are ready. I have other responsibilities to take care of. Turn it off when you are done."

Nacu left the room, and John was left there staring at a blank screen. Finally, he pushed the play button, and a video taken at the front gate began to play. He saw a blonde-haired woman in a blue skirt and white blouse. She looked familiar. She said, "Hello, John. My name is Jane Watkins. I am currently a reporter for the *Seattle Gazette*, and I have been looking for you for days. The last time we met, I had a knife in my belly and was bleeding badly until you saved me and healed me from my wounds. We had a very short conversation, and then I went to get help and told you to stick around, but you left before I could talk to you again. How rude. I know who you are, and I know you can do extraordinary things and have been helping people in this area for years. I am not interested in revealing who you are to the world, but you owe me a conversation and explanation.

"I have made reservations at the Pink Door in Seattle tomorrow night at 7:00 p.m. in my name. I know it seems a little presumptuous of me, but I would really like to see you. If you cannot, or won't, see me for any reason, then just call the Pink Door and cancel the reservations. I will make no further attempt to see you. Please don't stand me up. I am a friend and admirer of your work. If you choose not to see me, thanks for saving my life."

John was flabbergasted and speechless. He did not know what to say or what to do about the reservation. He then smiled and thought with everything that had happened in the last several days, *Why not?*

"General, we want to know why you authorized Second Infantry to move on Mount Rainier yesterday and gave the orders to investigate the legal scientific exploration of the volcano."

General Wade Eiling had visitors from the Department of Defense wanting answers. He was not pleased and could see that both the men were political types who didn't understand how things worked in the military even though they were from the government—straight from the secretary of defense's office in fact. They had introduced themselves as Malcolm James from the director's office of administration and management and Oscar Martinez from the director's office of program analysis and evaluation. He disliked the long titles the government types liked to have.

"I answer directly to the chairman of the Joint Chiefs of Staff, General Dempsey. Why didn't he call me? You guys came a long way for something that could have been handled over the phone."

Malcolm James replied, "The deputy secretary of defense asked us personally to come, but General Dempsey has been notified of our visit. We are only here to find the facts about the siege on the mountain."

The general explained, "I would hardly call it a siege. We simply detained a well-armed military group on the mountain until we verified who they were and their reason for gathering over one hundred armed men in a US National Park. I don't know where you got your information, but that was what happened."

Oscar Martinez asked, "How did you come to the decision to send the infantry to Mount Rainier, General?"

The general answered, "The park rangers reported gunfire and an explosion in the park near the trailer. Then they called back later to tell our office that they were mistaken. Leaving nothing to chance, I ordered a high-altitude surveillance of the area, and they reported the gathering of the military force. Having no memos or correspondence from the Department of Defense about a military exercise on the mountain, I decided to investigate. Captain McNair is finishing his report of the activities on the mountain, and I will file a report and send it to General Dempsey when I am finished."

Malcolm James explained, "The scientific study of the mountain was done with the right government permits and clearances, and the use of a security military force was authorized by the Department of Defense. Your men interfered with a legitimate operation and may have set us up for a legal suit."

General Eiling was losing his patience but remained calm. He said in a firm voice, "The Department of Defense answers to the secretary who answers to the president, who is the head of the Department of Justice. Let them handle my proper investigation of the incident on the mountain. Maybe next time you will let this office know so we don't interfere with any civilian-military activities authorized by the Department of Defense."

Malcolm James gritted his teeth and said, "Thanks for the civics lesson, General. We will be very interested in your full report when finished. Expect a communication from the Joint Chiefs of Staff later. The deputy secretary of defense will be in contact with your office also at the conclusion of our investigation."

The general thought, *They know more than they are telling me. Some VIP was pissed that we interrupted what he was doing on the mountain or is trying to hide something. He must have some pull in DC.* Then he said, "If you gentlemen are done, I have a military to run."

Malcolm James responded, "Yes, we are done here. Good day, General."

The general's aide showed the men out of his office.

Chapter 14

"David, we need to call the park at Mount Rainier and alert them to the danger. Things are happening very fast. There is some water runoff from several of the glaciers spotted by the locals hiking the mountain. One man near the town of Orting reported a lot of fast-running water. That can change to flood water running over thirty miles per hour very quickly."

Steven Ricker was talking to David Spencer about their findings from the recent volcanic activity on the mountain. They had been working for weeks to come to an educated conclusion about the possibility of an eruption of Mount Rainier. The University of Washington gave them an office to work out of and store their gear in. They worked with the Pacific Northwest Seismic Network and the US Geological Survey to help set the warning levels for all the Cascade volcanoes.

David replied, "Yes, seismic activity has increased tenfold from weeks previous, and with the water runoff, I am recommending we change the Volcano Hazards Program warning from green to orange. We should put everyone on watch alert as soon as possible. I will call the USGS and the park right now."

Steven agreed, "Yes, the USGS stations agree with your findings. I'll call the communities closest to the danger zone and my wife; it looks like we're not going home too soon."

The 2007–2008 expansion of real-time monitoring stations increased the number of continuous GPS (global positioning system) stations operating within Mount Rainier National Park from one to seven, the number of tiltmeters from zero to two, and the number of seismic stations from five to eight. It was one of the most extensive upgrades in volcanic monitoring in history. The idea was to give all the communities enough warning of an eruption or lahar flow with mud and water from the mountain.

David remarked, "Hope this is just a minor uprising of the mountain. I never thought I would see the possibility of an eruption in my lifetime."

It was late afternoon, and John was reconsidering his decision to see the woman. What was he doing there, and why was he seeing her? He didn't know her. Maybe she was playing him and had other motives for seeing him other than curiosity. He had been to the waterfront, enjoying the walk, and was headed back to the downtown area. He still had some time to cancel if he wanted to. It was a beautiful day after the rain showers; the air was clear, and the sun was out. John had enjoyed the solitude after the hectic events of the last couple of days. He had much to think about and paused at the waterfront to say a prayer that God would make things clear to him. John was confused and wanted guidance, but the one person he trusted most to help in times of need was not there.

John had gathered all the scrolls that represented Nathanial Tomar's life and put them in his study but had not touched them yet. It was too painful right now; he had to work this out somehow. He remembered that he always had a hard time reading Tomar's mind except for the surface thoughts because he was so disciplined. Only when he shared his meditation techniques did he open up. He lived his life, not by reading people's thoughts, but by judging their actions, words, and emotions. John's thoughts went back to the woman. He had made a vow to himself. He would not judge the woman using his powers. It would be just like normal people. He would get to know her like everyone else did. He would not read her mind without her permission. It was how Tomar met his mother in Chicago. They got to know each other the old-fashioned way, by just being with each other and observing each other's life. Tomar's words came back to him from years ago when he asked him how he came to know his mother and discovered she was the one for him.

He said to a young John, "She was kind and thoughtful of others and had the most beautiful smile. I loved to make her happy just to see her smile. I knew the love I had for her was returned by her eyes. She could never lie to me, even in jest; her eyes would betray her. Her body language told me that she cared deeply for the things that I did. She had an interest in me, but my interest was in her. I have had love before in my life, but none like her. She will be the last woman I will ever be with as a husband. One more thing, we were madly in love with you. It was the natural thing to make you my son when she became my wife. I miss her greatly."

I do too, and I miss you also, Dad, John thought to himself. He had walked farther downtown than he'd wanted to. He would have to double back to get to the restaurant. It was getting late. He saw a flower shop and thought, *Why not get some flowers?* He walked inside, ordered a bouquet of flowers, and paid for them. As they wrapped them in tissue, he looked at the clock. John had just enough time to walk to the restaurant by seven.

Jane had arrived at the restaurant early, which was unusual because she was rarely on time for anything; her friends were always teasing her about it. They had seated her outside per her request because it was a temperate day, very nice. The view from the outdoor deck was spectacular. The sun was going down, and the clouds in the sky painted the sunlight bright-yellow and orange and different hues of red. The clouds were outlined in purple and blue as they towered over the water in Elliott Bay. She was pleased to see the reservation was not canceled and anticipated his arrival any minute. It was an emotional search to find her savior.

She was admiring the view and looked around the restaurant. She recognized a tall man with blond hair walking to her table. Finally, he got close enough, and she noticed those fascinating blue eyes that she had seen the evening she was attacked. She fought back tears and took a drink of water to give her time to put her emotions in check.

He arrived at the table and said, "Jane Watkins, you look beautiful this evening."

Jane was wearing a dark-blue cocktail dress with slender straps that went over her shoulders and a modest top that sagged slightly in the middle. As she stood up, the dress clung to her hips to reveal a tiny waist. They embraced lightly, and John walked to her side to slide the chair under her as she sat down again.

Jane spoke. "You are one hard man to find. Thank you for meeting me tonight, John."

John was wearing a casual gray suit jacket with a light-green shirt and light-blue slacks. He sat down and said, "Sorry I left you that night. I was a little busy and did not want to talk to the authorities. They would not understand what I do."

By then, the waiter had arrived. He said, "We found a vase for the flowers you brought. May I set them on the table?"

"Yes, thank you for that. Ms. Watkins, would you like to start with some wine?"

Jane replied, "Please call me Jane. Yes, a red wine of your choice, and thank you for the flowers; they are lovely."

John glanced at the wine menu and ordered a red wine from the wine list. The waiter left to get a bottle for them. Their eyes met, and John was the first to speak.

"You are an extraordinary woman and an even more remarkable investigative reporter. How in the world did you find me out of millions of people in this area?"

"Well, it is a long story. With 20 percent talent and 80 percent luck. First, you did not cover your face quickly enough and let me get a glimpse of you. You told Jack Nash your first name, and Detective Jones is an old-school buddy of yours. You both graduated from college six years ago. You and your father gave an ancient spear and knife to the museum. And a truck driver named Charley said you saved his life like you did mine. That trek led me to your doorstep."

John smiled and said, "Sounds like 80 percent talent and determination and 20 percent luck. What drove you to find me, Jane?"

"You could save me from Nash and heal my wound, but the emotional trauma does not go away that easy. I was driven to see you. I wanted to expose you to start with, and then I realized you are a blessing to the community and exposing you would change the way you operate. You seem to work better without people's knowledge that you even exist. I could not bring myself to do that to you. Your story is too extraordinary. People would have a hard time believing there is a person of your talents. My motive changed. I just wanted to see you and thank you in person for what you do and saving my life."

John smiled and said, "You're welcome."

Just then, the waiter arrived with the bottle of wine and poured some into their wineglasses.

John said, "Have you looked at the menu? What would you like?"

John ordered the spaghetti dinner, and Jane ordered the lasagna meal.

After they ordered, Jane looked at John and asked, "I hope you believe me when I say that I wanted to thank you, but the reporter side of me has many questions. Can you answer a few for me?"

John watched her eyes and saw a sincere look of curiosity. He thought for a second and said, "Let's face it, Jane. You are an information junkie. The more you get, the more you want. It's in your nature, and it makes you a great reporter. You can't just have a little; you want the whole story. Every jot and tittle. Once we start, how do I stop revealing myself to you?"

Jane looked at the bay and then back at John. She said, "John, you are the most remarkable person I have ever met. Your selflessness goes beyond your abilities. I want to get to know the person you are, not just what you can do. I don't think of you as the main attraction in a circus but as a real, live human being. I would just like to get to know you. Is that possible? Is there a way that can happen?"

John was not himself because of recent events. He thought for a moment and said, "I recently witnessed the death of someone I loved very much. I need some time to mourn that loss. Then perhaps we can explore possibilities."

Jane gave a look of sympathy and replied, "I am sorry for your loss. I certainly don't want to intrude, and I so appreciate you seeing me tonight."

She reached into her purse and pulled out a piece of paper. She wrote something on it and then gave it to John. "I don't want to exert any pressure on you or give you a time table. Take as long as you like. This is my number. Call me when you want to talk possibilities. Perhaps we can finish the evening with small talk and enjoy our meal. It is a beautiful evening."

John put the paper in his coat pocket and smiled. He said, "It certainly is."

They talked weather and flowers and other things and just enjoyed the evening together. After dinner, it was dark, and John walked her outside. He offered to go with her to her car, but Jane said, "Thank you for a very pleasant time and dinner, but I will be fine." Then she reached up and kissed him on the cheek. "I hope to see you again. Good-bye, John."

She turned and walked away, and John watched her disappear around the block. Then he smiled and walked away.

"This is KOIN 6 Eyewitness News where we are watching out for you. This just in: if you are planning a trip to Mount Rainier in Washington soon, you might want to change your plans. The US Geological Survey has just issued a warning about volcanic activity on Mount Rainier and in the national park. They have changed the Volcano Hazards Program warning from green to orange. With the mountain only sixty miles from Tahoma and the Seattle area, this is a major concern for those living in the area. The smaller communities' populations amount to well over a hundred thousand people. They are in direct danger of an eruption or lahar flow. The flood of mud and water will be moving very fast if the volcano heats up the glaciers. Here is Professor Oliver Alexander from geological sciences at the University of Oregon to answer some questions about the possibility of an eruption on Mount Rainier."

Jacob was in a hotel room, watching the news in Portland, Oregon, near his offices there. He turned the sound down on the television and picked up his phone. He dialed Professor George Ohm, who was in another room in the hotel.

The professor answered the phone. "Hello?"

"Have you seen the evening news?"

The professor recognized Jacob's voice and said, "Yes, I saw the report on the mountain."

Jacob asked, "Will it erupt?"

"That's hard to say. I am no longer in control of the grid system we installed and can't monitor its progress. The mountain is in control now. I know there is a huge pocket of lava near the surface on the west side that could heat up the glaciers and cause floods of mud and water, or it could come to the surface and erupt with lava and still cause the glaciers to melt. The lava is situated toward the more populated areas, so the chance of property damage is high but a great loss of life, probably not. There are too many variables to be certain. The mountain could calm down and not flare up for a hundred more years."

Jacob smiled and said to the professor, "I think whatever it does, we can use it for our benefit, and Starr Enterprises will be there for the community. Fear is very powerful in persuading people to see things our way. Yes, I will correspond with the locals and offer my services to build their trust. There is an old saying, 'How do you eat an elephant?' We will do it 'one bite at a time.' I will instruct the department heads of Starr Corp to assist in any way they can."

Professor Ohm reminded Jacob, "Don't forget there is a group of people who know what we tried to do. They may have to be reckoned with."

"Yes, reckoned with or destroyed, and I prefer the latter. Don't worry, Professor, I have not forgotten them at all. Knowledge is power, and I will know more about them soon. Yes, very soon."

John got home late, and Nacu greeted him in the kitchen. He asked, "How did your walk downtown go? Did it help you sort things out? You have been gone all day."

John looked at Nacu and answered, "It was nice to do nothing for a change and reflect on what happened recently. Plus, I met a beautiful woman and had dinner with her."

"You saw her, didn't you? The woman in the video?"

John chuckled and said, "Yes, I did. She is very nice and wants to see me again."

Nacu reminded John, "She is the media, and they are not our friends. Tomar always said that. We should work under the radar, away from public scrutiny. Reporters are the worst."

"Believe me, Nacu; I know that, and I told her nothing important, but she knew me and my friends and what I have done in the past very well, and she has not used it against me. She said she never would and that she just wanted to thank me."

"Well, did she thank you? And are you going to see her again?"

John looked down and said, "I really don't know right now. I told her I was in mourning and could not decide to see her again at this time. She accepted that, and we had a pleasant evening just being with each other. She gave me her phone number and walked to her car after dinner. I walked a little more near the water and then came home."

"What a day you've had. You need to know that Albert has been in his laboratory since you left. He only had a small breakfast all day. I was about to check on him. Would you like the honor, John?"

John looked at Nacu and said, "Sure, I'll check on him. Good night, Nacu."

John walked to the backyard and then went to the area to his left. Professor Albert Hughes's laboratory was adjacent to the house. He walked in. The professor was looking at a computer screen. John made enough noise while entering the lab that the professor noticed him, and before John could say a word, he said, "John! Just the man I want to talk to. I have some extraordinary news on two counts that you have to know."

John walked toward the professor and said, "It's late; will it wait until tomorrow?"

The professor looked right at John and said, "I think not. You need to hear what I have found out."

John conceded and said, "All right, Albert. What do you have?"

"Well, remember I had Phillip gather a few things from the site of the last conflict with Jacob and his men? One of the things I asked him for was any remnant of Tomar that was left when the laser hit him. The laser light could not have covered his whole body, even at the widest area. Phillip left me a note in the evidence bag that said there was nothing left of Tomar. There was not a piece of clothing or body part in the area of the laser blast. That is impossible. There should be something."

"Professor, I was there; I saw him vanish right before my eyes. That laser could vaporize steel. Perhaps it consumed what was left."

"We did laser tests at the university, and there was always something left out of the fire zone. The laser had an effective zone of twelve to twenty-four inches. There should have been something left of his body."

John looked puzzled and said, "What does this mean, Professor?"

He smiled and said, "If I am right, it means Nathanial Tomar may still be alive. You remember that you told me that around volcanoes there can be dimensional temporal distortions, and you would look for one of those when you went onto the mountain? Well, I believe that Tomar was close to one when the great power and heat generated by the laser opened the portal between dimensions and Tomar was swept into another world."

This apparently surprised John. He asked, "Albert, let me get my head around what you are saying. It is possible when the laser was fired, that Tomar might have survived and was swept into another dimension?"

The professor sighed and replied, "Yes, John, that is what I am saying. I need to interview Phillip when he comes back for more information, but that is my belief."

John looked at the ground with tears in his eyes and said, "You don't know how much I want to believe you. If it is true, I need to talk to Eli or Enoch; they may have a way to get to him, or he could be trying to find his way back right now."

John kept his emotions in check because he knew he could not take the disappointment if the professor was wrong, but he remained hopeful and said, "Thank you for giving me hope that he survived. I want it to be true, but you said when I entered the lab that there were two things of extraordinary news you wanted to tell me. What is the other?"

The professor looked at the computer screen and said, "I want to show you something on the computer."

They walked over to the screen, and John saw several graphs with numbers on them. Each was a separate specimen. The numbers were in columns and rows and had similar two-digit numbers.

John was really confused. He asked, "What am I looking at, Professor?"

"I had Phillip take DNA samples from all the superhumans at the site. This one here is Jacob, and this one is you. You and he share over 70 percent of the same numbers. I was surprised and came across it quite by accident."

John looked at the screen again and said, "What does this mean?"

The professor answered, "It means that you and Jacob share the same biological mother and father. There is a mathematical certainty of 99.99 percent. You and he are brothers."

Jacob was entering the part of the airport where his jet was parked. Legion was driving an SUV and would be at the plane in a couple of minutes.

Jacob told Legion, "I want you to stay with Professor Ohm and help him and Centurion with salvaging what we can from the trailer and other equipment from the mountain. I will call you later when I need you in Chicago."

Legion responded with a muffled, "Yes, sir," because of the fracture of his jaw and the pain in his broken ribs. The doctor who had treated him called it a simple fracture, put a couple of wires in the jaw to keep it in position, and prescribed him a soft food diet. Legion made a face of disapproval but did not question Jacob's orders.

As they were arriving at the plane, Jacob's phone rang. He looked at the number and saw it was a number from the Chicago area. Very few people had his private number, so he was surprised when it rang. He answered it. "Yes?"

It was Drina Winters, Jacob's nanny in the Starr household. She also ran the affairs of the mansion for his father, Jeremiah Starr. She was to the point with Jacob and said, "Jacob, your father is dying."

Jacob, with very little emotion, replied, "His doctors can't save him this time?"

Drina answered, "No, he is dying, only a few days to live. You need to see him."

Jacob inhaled deeply and said, "Well, he lived his life without me; I think he can die without me just fine."

Drina sounded disappointed when she said, "Jacob, you need to come; he is asking for you. He wants to talk to you. Please come."

"Nanny, you are a hard one to say no to. I will be there as soon as I get back to Chicago."

Drina sounded relieved. "Thank you, Jacob; it will be good to see you. Bye."

Jacob replied, "Good-bye, Nanny Drina."

Jacob entered the jet plane and left for Chicago.

Chapter 15

The mansion was located north of Chicago near Lake Michigan. The Starr family had lived here for over one hundred years, and the estate was one of the largest in the area. Jacob had just arrived, and his driver was navigating the roadway that led to the mansion. The house was built with brick on the lower and upper floor. White colonial pillars were highlighting the white wood trim and the large windows with a massive double door which was also white. He was here at the request of Drina Winters who administered the estate for his father. She called Jacob and convinced him to see his father before he dies. Jacob had recovered sufficiently from the ordeal on the mountain in Washington State, but he was still dealing with the unsettling circumstances. He was wearing dark gray slacks with brown shoes and a gray sports jacket with light blue shirt and no tie. He walked into the house and Drina met him inside near the stairway.

"I am so glad you are here Jacob your father is very sick, and the doctor does not know how much longer he has." Nanny Drina looked concerned and tired from the added stress managing the declining health of the master of the house along with her other daily duties. Jacob looked at the woman who had raised him in place of a birth mother. His look garnered the respect that came from being on the receiving end of her service to the family for many years. She was about five foot six and had her medium length gray hair put up with a modest dress nothing fancy. Her eyes were dark green with a hint of blue. She was a strong woman who handled her responsibilities well. Initially, he seemed indifferent and unemotional then Jacob smiled slightly and said to her. "Nanny Drina it is good to see you. I am pleased that you are still here in service to the family." He paused for a moment, then remembered why he was here and said. "May I go right in to see him? Is there anything about his condition I should know?"

She returned his smile and said. "He knows that he does not have much time left. When he realized this fact the first thing he wanted to do is talk to you; the second was to send a message to the council of which I am not privy. I will let him know you are here. I am sure he will see you right away." Drina went up the stairs to check on Jeremiah Starr and let him know his son was here to see him.

Jacob was left alone at the base of the stairs. He looked around the mansion. He had spent his childhood here and ran up, and down these very stairs many years ago, the base of the stairs was about 15 feet wide and narrowed as you walked upward. The handrail circled inward and at the bottom reached out in opposite directions. As you ascended the stairs they narrowed and split in two directions at a wall; one stairway left and one right where they continued to the living quarters and bedrooms. On the wall at the end of the first run of stairs Jeremiah Starr's oil painting portrait hung. Within moments Drina came down the stairs and informed Jacob his father would see him. Then she said. "He is weak and very tired don't excite him too much. He is heavily medicated but still alert and responsive. You know the way."

Jacob walked up the stairs to the master bedroom and opened the door. As he walked in, he noticed the room was semi-dark with the curtain partially closed. It took his eyes a moment to adjust to the lack of light in the place. He walked toward the large king-sized bed which had a wood bed frame with a plain white bed sheet and quilt and a thick brown leather headboard. Jeremiah was lying down with his eyes closed. He was a shadow of the man he had seen just weeks ago; his eyes were sunk back in his eye sockets, and his flesh color was pale. His hair was thinning and almost all white. He was a very slender version of the strong man Jacob knew as his father.

As Jacob walked toward the bed Jeremiah opened his eyes suddenly, then he tried to set up but was not successful. His voice was weak, but he managed to say. "Son, you made it. I am glad to see you. We have much to discuss and little time to resolve our differences."

Jacob lowered his eyebrows and replied. "Differences? We never had a life in common to have differences. The teachers and mentors were more of a father to me than you. You had very little time for me except to set in the background and criticize my actions. I could not please you."

"Jacob, I knew what you were capable of and had to push for you to reach your potential. You still have more to learn and accomplish. There is much more to gain for our people and yourself."

"That's OK; I have plans of my own. I really don't care what you have for me. I will be successful beyond your wildest dreams and benefit our people and myself in the process. I have great power in my grasp and have key people in high places in governments and business to aid me in whatever I do."

"Son, I know of your failure on the mountain and how close you came to losing your life up there in the forest. I know what you tried to accomplish and what you are trying to do to be accepted as a leader worldwide."

Jacob looked surprised and distressed, and then he replied.

"Jeremiah Starr, you know I will kill the mole in my organization that reported that to you. Even now you monitor my actions and critique what I do."

"Jacob, before you tear your organization apart looking for that man, listen to me what I have to say."

Jacob shook his head left to right then calmed himself and said. "Ok old man, you have my attention. Tell me what you have to say."

Jacob looked at his father with disdain but listened to him talk. "I never told you the whole story about your mother. You know her name was Mary, and she died when you were a baby, but you don't understand she was handpicked because of her DNA profile and physical features matched what our scientist said would produce that perfect child, the ultimate in human development. Our people have prophesied for one hundred generations about this particular child. They engineered human DNA to bring about the Omni child. He would lead humanity to man's age of prosperity. It was his destiny. That prediction you know, but what you don't know is that Mary gave birth to two children that day. Fraternal twins were born just moments apart, your brother first then you. John and Jacob the Omni Twins had such potential, but then everything changed.

"On the eight day after your birth you were taken by the doctors to be circumcised, and then an implant was put in your neck near the right ear. It could monitor your vitals and transmit conversations within the range of your hearing. I used it to keep a close watch on your activities and keep you safe. It also sent me a signal where you were at all times. It is still active and operational. That is how I know about the conflict on the mountain."

Jacob was infuriated and said. "You're despicable, controlling my life was not enough. You had to invade my privacy and know everything I did. I ought to kill you right where you lay."

Jeremiah coughed and said. "Go ahead kill me do me the favor of a quick death, but you won't hear the rest of the story. There is much more." Jacob calmed his rage for the moment and conceded to hear the rest. Jeremiah sensed this and continued telling the story.

"When the doctors went to get your brother to do the same to John, they found he and your mother were gone. She stole the child and left. We looked for months to find her and the child. You and your brother were precious to me, but with the loss of John, you became the primary hope of our people. I still had you, and I was not going to lose you. I was determined to watch over you and give you the best mentors and guidance. Your power is like no one I have ever seen. There is nothing you can't do."

Jacob interrupted. "It is a little late to flatter me or pat yourself on the back for the father of the year. What happened to Mary and John? Do you know where they are?"

"Mary was found months later at a restaurant in Chicago. One of my men drugged her with a special poison, and then he tried to bring her to me, so I could question her but before he could give her the antidote to revive her; Mary's companion attacked my men and broke the bottle that had the medicine to revive her. The companion grabbed her body and disappeared. We never saw him or her again. We searched for days. Without the antidote, she must be dead. Your brother was lost to me now, but I still had you. You must put your feelings aside and listen. There is much more I have to say." Jeremiah just ran out of breath and gasped for air and rested for the moment.

Jacob slowly shook his head from side to side and said.

"Jeremiah, your failure is complete. Not only did you lose my brother you lost me a long time ago. We have nothing between us. I only exist to further the goals of you and my people. According to your twisted sense of family, I should welcome what you have to say and your plans for me."

Just then Jacob's phone went off. He pulled the cell phone from his pocket and saw it was Trevor, his military contract leader. He left him with Legion his driver and muscle to clean up the sight on Mount Rainier and move everything back to Portland Oregon after the conflict on the mountain. He hit the auto-respond which sent a text to Trevor saying he would call right back. He looked back at his father who was beginning to cough and wheeze. He did not know how much more he could take of this conversation.

Suddenly the nurse came in and interrupted them by saying. "I am sorry his vitals are too high he may have a seizure you must leave right now. You can come back later. I have to give him some medicine." Jeremiah's coughing and breathing was getting worse, so Jacob left and went down to the lobby. Drina met him there and said.

Jacob, are you finished with your father? Is he ok?

Jacob responded.

"He is not doing well right now the nurse is attending to him. I will be back later to finish with him, but right now I need to call someone and see my surgeon about a problem I have. You and I need to talk later; please excuse me for now." Then he walked out the front door and called Trevor.

Jane Watkins was about to retire for the night. She had not slept for over eighteen hours. She had been covering the eruption of Mount Rainier, which spewed ash and lava for about ten hours out of the west side just below the summit. The resulting lava melted most of the glaciers and sent vast amounts of water and mud to the lower communities. The authorities were still trying to figure the total damage and death toll in the area. She was the spearhead for the Gazette's news stories and authored a lot of the front-page articles of the paper. Jane had been in the regions that were the most onerous, and she was very distressed by the devastation. She worked diligently, trying to get the whole story about the tragedy. Finally, her editor, Fred Hembeck pulled her from the area and sent her home to get some rest.

Jane was sitting at her desk, which was located just a few feet from her bed, which looked very inviting to her body. Jane was exhausted both mentally and physically, but she pulled out a personal journal she had not used in months and began writing:

"Dear Diary,

I am tired and should just go to bed, but I had to write a few things down while they are fresh in my mind. It turns out my objection to my editors putting me on the story about Mount Rainier was not fair to them, and the assignment resulted in one of the biggest stories in Washington State history. The tallest volcano in Washington woke up and reminded us she was a threat to the community. While it could have been much worse, it was terrible enough; many people lost their lives, perhaps hundreds, we don't know yet. Some are still stranded, awaiting rescue efforts to free them in isolated areas. This event is a real tragedy, like none I have ever seen.

Just over three days ago, everything was right with the world. My search to find the mystery man in my life was over. I even found where he lives. He was everything I hoped he would be. He is the most exciting man I have ever met, and I think I am falling for him. My infatuation with the miracle man in armor who saved me has turned into genuine affection toward the man I met in the restaurant. I want to be with him. I hope he contacts me again, but I don't know if I can wait much longer. I found him and then let him go much too quickly, but now is not the time to worry about that.

I have no doubt he is rescuing as many people as he can in the tragedy, so it will have to wait. We both have our calling and must do what we can to help. Perhaps I will see him again later, but I am too tired to think anymore. I must rest; tomorrow's another day."

After writing the last words, she fell into bed and dropped off into a deep sleep.

Appendix

Excerpts from the Journal of Professor Albert Hughes, documenting his investigation of the Genesis Project

The Genesis Project
Log Entry 1.1

I decided to stay after the remarkable claims Nathanial Tomar made to me in his library the other night, and I am glad I did. My time in the Northwest should be interesting, from what I saw yesterday. I witnessed a man run over three hundred miles per hour and a woman who can jump vertically over twenty feet and communicate with animals. I saw a man who can throw flames from his hands and fly by heating the air around him and another woman who can control kinetic energy and shows some ability to see the future. I saw a young man lift fifty thousand pounds over his head.

I met a remarkable young man with heightened senses, telekinesis, superstrength, and the surprising ability to read minds. Plus, there is a substance that causes these abilities to develop in people, and it is mine to study, provided by my benefactor, Nathanial Tomar. I have some in the laboratory and will use what knowledge I have to examine this substance, including forensic science. I must learn how it changes in different environments, plus what it does when it contacts human tissue. I will use every test I can to come to a logical and—I hope—accurate conclusion.

I have ordered some new equipment that Nathanial Tomar is kind enough to provide in my endeavor to unlock the secrets of the substance. I have decided to name this substance the Genesis Factor. That is because this is taking us back to the beginning of the understanding of what is possible in the world of science. I will try to adhere to the strict standards of scientific examination. I will use this medium of log entries for statements and conclusions of what I have discovered from time to time. It will not be as technical as my daily logs so the laymen can understand. I feel privileged and appreciate my chance to explore the Genesis Factor and will treat the study with the diligence it deserves.

The Genesis Project
Log Entry 3.1

Phillip Black is the first to be examined in more depth. I find that when he is in a state of hyperspeed, his mind and nervous system operate at least a hundred times faster than a normal healthy person's. Phillip describes it as seeing everything around him in ultraslow motion. His maximum speed so far in an open area is Mach 1, which is 761 miles per hour, but my test showed that he is capable of reaching Mach 2. The problem in reaching these high speeds is twofold. The aerodynamics of the human body are not designed for that kind of speed, and the normal human body cannot store enough fuel in carbohydrates to generate the energy needed for a 185-pound man to run that fast.

With the first problem involving the aerodynamics of the human body, we put him in a wind tunnel on a treadmill and shot tiny dust particles in the air to observe what happened when he reached high speeds. At one hundred miles per hour, the computer showed the outline of air being pushed around his body in a much more aerodynamic way. At two hundred miles per hour and even more and at three hundred miles per hour, the air particles showed the outline of something that resembled a missile and not that of a man. The conclusion is that Phillip subconsciously creates a force field around himself to protect him from the friction of the wind.

The second problem: Where does the energy come from to sustain that speed? He must be tapping into some energy around him that is solar, kinetic, or atomic; otherwise, what he is doing is impossible, and he clearly proves that it is possible. All the subjects have this same problem: where does the energy come from for them to perform their superhuman feats? Perhaps that will become clear in more tests of these extraordinary people and my direct study of the substance I call the Genesis Factor.

Each person I have interviewed developed his or her powers before coming to this area with the substance, so if the Genesis Factor is responsible, then there must be other areas of the world where it is in the water table and somehow was imbibed by these young people. I will cover that in detail in a later log.

The Genesis Project
Log Entry 5.1

Carol Saboya is a remarkable study. As a person, she is a doctor of veterinary medicine and contributed to the studies of animal life in the Amazon for the University of Brasilia. Her mental ability to communicate with animals is a study in itself. It has revealed that some lower forms of life in the animal kingdom operate at an instinctual level only, but higher primates, dolphins, and other mammals have developed a rudimentary language. She was studying that when Nathan Tomar asked her to join the group. She maintains her studies here in her own laboratory on the grounds. She is very intelligent; I will measure her IQ soon.

On the physical level, she is in perfect health. Her bone density is three times that of a normal person. Her muscle tissue function is faster and stronger than that of a well-trained athlete. She can lift six hundred pounds over her head, run over thirty miles per hour, and jump twenty feet in the air. Her motor skills and nervous system work three times faster than normal. Her hearing and vision are well above normal. Her stamina is extraordinary; she can operate at a high level of activity for over three hours before fatigue begins.

Again, she developed some degree of super ability before coming here to the complex, so there must be a source of the Genesis Factor in the water she drank somewhere in Brazil. She has very fast healing abilities. Wounds heal in hours, not days. With her permission, I injected her with the cold virus, and she developed no symptoms of a cold. She said she has not been sick in years. Hand-to-eye coordination is well above normal, and she has the fighting skills of a black belt in any martial art with twice the speed. My assumption is she has been taking the substance for years. Checking the DNA of all the superpeople to see if there is something in common with them all and how it has changed from normal DNA.

The Genesis Project
Log Entry 6.1

Aiko Sakura was the next in the study. Somehow, she has the ability to change energy used around her to force. She can convert the kinetic energy of an attacker into a force and repel the attacker backward. Objects thrown at her, she can repel at will, and she has absorbed some energy from electrical lighting and sunlight and can use it in a burst of pure force, which she can maintain for short periods of time. I am working with her to change other forms of energy into something else constructive, like magnetic energy or electrical and gravitational energy. She has shown promise in this area.

Like the others, she is in excellent physical shape and is able to outperform trained athletes in all physical tasks. Her abilities enhance the fact that she is a martial arts expert from her time in Japan. She is a much more formidable opponent than her small size would suggest. She is able to handle four-hundred-pound weights very easily and work out with them on a regular basis. She also is able to operate at a high level of physical activity for over three hours before fatigue sets in.

Even more interesting than her powers with energy and her physical prowess is her ability to see the future. She says when she closes her eyes, she can see people and events before they happen. I tested that by asking her to identify playing cards that I would show her within thirty seconds, and she identified all 100 percent correctly. The farther the time period before she saw the card, the less accurate she was; at ten minutes, she was 95 percent accurate, twenty minutes 80 percent, and so on. She told me she had predicted things in the past that did not happen exactly as she saw in the future but were similar in prediction. She explained that the more distantly she looked into the future, the cloudier it got in her mind. Perhaps she is looking into the time stream and the farther she looks, the harder things are to see. In time, there are many variables that can change the future that is possible at the moment. However it works, it is very interesting to speculate. She is a remarkable study. All these young people are very special in their own way.

The Genesis Project
Log Entry 7.1

Hiroki Sakura is the brother to Aiko Sakura, and he is the firstborn of these fraternal twins. He is able to generate extreme heat in objects. He can melt steel in a matter of seconds and heat the air around himself to make his body lighter than air and simulate flight at great speeds. He is able to project flames from his body; where the fuel comes from for doing this, I don't know. It is a mystery I hope to solve in the future. How he keeps his flesh from burning is also puzzling. He allowed me to use a cutting torch on his hand, and the flames were driven around his fingers and did not burn his flesh. His hand was cool to the touch also. The source of the heat must be similar to the way Aiko converts energy to force. In my test, he has generated heat of over three thousand degrees. I really don't have a proper place to test beyond that right now, but Nathan Tomar is working on building a superoven that can handle over eleven thousand degrees Fahrenheit.

He is in great physical shape, like the others tested. His strength, speed, and endurance are way beyond the normal range. He is an expert in martial arts, which is also enhanced by his superior physical body. I saw him lift over five hundred pounds and operate at high physical activity for over three hours before fatigue set in. Don't know how far his physical abilities can be developed beyond that right now, but I will monitor all tested for improvement as time goes on. He, like everyone tested, heals very fast—in hours not days. I am amazed how much care he takes not to hurt other people when he generates great heat. He is disciplined in all his actions and seems very protective of his sister. He is another remarkable product of the Genesis Factor.

The Genesis Project
Log Entry 8.1

Samuel Touré was the first to demonstrate a true feat of strength. I watched him lift fifty thousand pounds over his head. His body is built for strength, but he can exceed the limits of his six-foot-eight-inch, 255-pound frame when he needs to. It seems to be triggered through the adrenaline generated by the task at hand. The greater the task or threat, the greater the strength generated. Nathan Tomar told the story of him saving a man in a construction hole with a truck on his body in his home country of the Republic of Guinea in Africa. He lifted a twenty-ton truck off the man and saved his life. His healing rate is remarkably fast. Small cuts heal in seconds and larger wounds in minutes. He is very agile for a person his size, and his agility and speed are increased when he is exerting himself.

The most remarkable observation of his feats of strength is that he gains mass and becomes harder to hurt, almost invulnerable to harm. His molecular structure changes right before my eyes. When he exerts his strength, his bone density increases. So does his weight and size. Where the extra mass comes from is unknown and another mystery of these special people. The more I study the effects of the Genesis Factor, the more questions it generates. After I have examined in depth all the superpowered people, I will look at the substance itself and see if there is a clue I am missing. I must continue in this astounding work by myself. I cannot contact any colleagues about my findings.

The Genesis Project
Log Entry 9.1

John Tomar is next. He is the most powerful and talented of all the superpeople. I will deal with each ability one by one. First is his ability to heal; he heals the fastest of all the people tested. Flesh regenerates in a matter of seconds. Veins and muscle also regenerate very quickly. What is more remarkable is the fact that he can heal others with his touch when they are injured. I don't know the limitation of his healing abilities, but there are limits. He said when he first realized he had this ability, he went to the hospital and touched as many people as he could without bringing attention to himself. After about four serious injuries or illnesses, he was spent emotionally and physically and needed some time to recover. So he decided not to do that anymore and deal with others on a one-to-one basis.

John's body, like the others', is in perfect health. He ran five miles at speeds of thirty miles per hour, and his heart rate and blood pressure were below normal. I have not tested his strength yet, but I saw him playing at the weight machine with five thousand pounds while having some fun with Samuel, so it is far beyond normal. No one in the group can subdue him in hand-to-hand; it is as if he knows what they are doing before they do it. That brings us to his mental abilities. He has somehow been able to concentrate brain waves beyond his body to move things, create force fields, and lift great objects with his mind. It seems to be limited to line of sight. I have not tested the limit of this power or the maximum distance of effectiveness yet. He was able to stop the flight of a .38-caliber bullet in a test session aimed at a target. The ability works on all objects, not just metal, so magnetism is not the source. It looks like true telekinesis, which I thought did not exist.

His mental abilities include reading minds and recognizing people's personal thoughts. He can read the conscious surface thoughts very easily, but deeper thoughts require more time and intrude in the other's thought patterns. With this ability, he can suggest the subject of his mental probe do something not of his or her own volition. He can induce sleep and influence emotion or revisit a traumatic memory. The tests I have done show that he is very disciplined in this area, careful not to damage the mind of another and cause trauma that would affect the person permanently. It is by far his most powerful and dangerous ability to humans. I could spend a lifetime studying this ability but have other things to work on with the Genesis Factor.

In conclusion, in my study of these superpeople, I cannot tell the source of their powers without examining the substance itself and how it changes them and makes them into something very super. It is like the comics we read as kids of superheroes and their feats. My study continues.

The Genesis Project
Log Entry 13.1

My preliminary check of the substance I have called "the Genesis Factor" has identified it as foreign to the earth. The spectroscopic analysis shows a molecular structure unlike any I have ever seen. Further checks with the mass spectrometer show some hydrogen and carbon, but the way the molecules are integrated with atomic particles is very complicated, and I am still plotting the molecular structure to help me understand it. There seem to be missing pieces of the puzzle in the atomic map I am trying to put together. The electromagnetic meter shows no electromagnetic radiation. The Geiger counter shows no radiation from the substance. The molecular structure is the key in the study.

When the substance is placed in water, it produces light—yellow to orange light, depending on the refraction of the water. This is a mystery to me. I am sure it is not the same as bioluminescent organisms, like those found in the sea, because the chemicals in the water after saturation are not the same as in sea water. At first, the light favors the infrared light visually, and then, after several hours in the water, it begins to become more yellow, like Tomar explained is in the cave of origin.

While I don't trust the scientific studies of Dr. Wilhelm Reich in the 1930s and his discovery of orgone energy or the so-called life-force energy, I found an experimental life-force meter in the lab and turned it on. The reading went off the scale on any setting or sensitivity around the substance. Reich was discredited because of his insistence that orgone energy exists, and he claimed that orgone energy was omnipresent and promoted life. Reich died on November 3, 1957, in the federal penitentiary at Lewisburg, Pennsylvania, where he was sent for criminal contempt. His selling of devices that he claimed could heal any medical disorder was stopped by the courts. I really don't know what this meter is reading, so I don't know what to make of the reads and will stay with the more conventional scientific study.

As for a scientific conclusion, I need more information for that. I am working diligently to unlock the secrets behind the Genesis Factor and hope to have more meaningful conclusions in the next log. More tests must be done.

The Genesis Project
Log Entry 20.1

Nathan Tomar once told me not to think of what is impossible but to think of what is possible. I find myself in a world where there are no limits. What I understood before is no longer valid scientific thought. We are dealing with dimensions I did not know existed. This is abstract science and goes beyond $E = mc^2$. The potential here is godlike, perhaps the secrets that God has hidden from us since creation. We were made for greater things than building the pyramids. This substance, called the Genesis Factor, unlocks the human potential, not by mutations, which are rarely beneficial, but by restoring the human body and psychic abilities to what was intended. Evolution has it wrong; mankind with all our advances cannot bring prosperity to the human state of despair and suffering. The human being stays the same or gets worse; there is not a utopian future in science alone.

We can help, but all our help is only marginal. The average world age at death is 67.2. I know you have to factor the human condition in the poor countries, and that is part of the problem. Men have tried to bring the age of prosperity and health only to fall to greed and personal interest. There has to be more to life and greater purpose, or why are we born?

This study has shown me that there is a force for good in this world, and I think that this entity is responsible for the Genesis Factor. Nathan Tomar has shown me through his testimony that he was chosen to guard the substance from man's greed, and he has done a wonderful job. His faith and life speak to me of God-given purpose. His respect for life and love for others teach me there is a better way to live my life. I am dedicated to the ideals he portrayed and lived. I will continue the study of the substance Nathan called the "water of life" and see where God will take me in understanding.

Where Nathan is right now, I do not know, but I believe he was not killed in the attack by Professor Ohm and is fighting his way back to us with as much passion as he lived in his life. Whatever his fate, I am glad I met him and that he introduced the Genesis Factor to me and trusted me enough to let me study it. I hope to see him soon.

Please join us in the continuing story *The Struggle: Book Two of the Genesis Project Series*, a new novel from the author W. B. Stiles, in print soon.

Printed in the United States
By Bookmasters